'I see you've m[...]
Mark said.

And that, Kirsty thou[...]
truly in my place. La[...]

Whatever warmth and welcome there had
been in the doctor's lean brown face as they'd
sat together that afternoon had gone. All his
earlier hostility was there, and more, Kirsty
realised, dismayed.

Elisabeth Scott was born in Scotland, but has lived in South Africa for many years. Happily married, with four children and grandchildren, she has always been interested in reading and writing about medical instances. Her middle daughter is a midwifery sister, and is Elisabeth's consultant on both medical authenticity and on how nurses feel and react. Her daughter wishes she met more doctors like the ones her mother writes about!

Recent titles by the same author:

OUTBACK DOCTOR
THE RELUCTANT HEART

LAURA'S NURSE

BY
ELISABETH SCOTT

MILLS & BOON

*All the characters in this book have no existence outside the imagina-
tion of the author, and have no relation whatsoever to anyone bearing
the same name or names. They are not even distantly inspired by any
individual known or unknown to the author, and all the incidents are
pure invention.*

*MILLS & BOON, the Rose Device and
LOVE ON CALL are trademarks of the publisher.
Harlequin Mills & Boon Limited,
Eton House, 18-24 Paradise Road, Richmond, Surrey TW9 1SR
This edition published by arrangement with Harlequin Enterprises B.V.*

© Elisabeth Scott 1995

ISBN 0 263 79061 4

*Set in Times 10 on 10½ pt. by
Rowland Phototypesetting Limited
Bury St Edmunds, Suffolk*

03-9505-55943

Made and printed in Great Britain

CHAPTER ONE

You didn't have favourite patients, Kirsty knew that. And she certainly didn't give Laura Barnard any more of her time or her attention than she gave to any of her other patients on Women's Surgical.

But she did have to admit—only to herself—that she couldn't help feeling there was a special bond between herself and the young South African girl.

It was almost three months since Laura's accident, and of course that was a long time for a patient to be in the surgical ward at St Luke's.

Kirsty had just come on duty, the day Laura had been brought to the ward on a trolley, straight from Theatre.

'Car accident,' Sister Maclean had explained tersely, when she'd come in to check that Kirsty and the young first-year nurse had got the bed ready. 'Fracture of the shaft of the femur—the fracture has been reduced, and she'll have a cast, and Mr Martin wants her in traction.' She'd inspected the traction frame, and nodded her approval.

'Now, Staff,' she'd said briskly, 'your gastric resection in Number Five is having problems with dumping syndrome again. See what you can do to persuade her that it really will help her if she lies in the position you put her in!'

Kirsty hadn't quite been sure how Mrs Jones had become 'her' gastric resection, but she'd gone off to persuade the old lady, once again, that the semi-recumbent position would help her to digest her food, and it would be wise to stay that way. She'd reminded Mrs Jones that the operation to treat her duodenal ulcer had been an extensive one, and she would recover sooner if she did as she was told. Straight talking, she had found, worked best with this old lady.

'Thanks, lass,' Mrs Jones said cheerfully and unrepentantly. 'I hope Sister wasn't too hard on you; it's just that I get restless, and I forget, and there I go again. Oh, here's your new patient.'

Kirsty and the young theatre nurse moved the unconscious girl to the bed with the traction frame, and Mr Martin, the orthopaedic surgeon, adjusted it.

'I've ordered a further transfusion, Sister,' the surgeon explained as Sister Maclean joined them. 'There was fairly extensive damage to soft tissue and muscle, severe displacement of bone fragments, and extensive blood loss.'

He shook his head.

'No respect for cars, young folks nowadays,' he said. 'Another two girls in the same accident, but they're the lucky ones; they'll be out in a couple of days. This lassie, now, will be with us for quite a while. She was in the passenger's seat, of course.'

The girl in the bed was still unconscious. She looked very young, Kirsty thought. Fair hair, and fair-skinned, but even now, when she was so pale, there was a golden tone to her skin, a memory of the sunshine of her home.

Poor kid, Kirsty thought, having a bad car accident like this, so far from her family.

'Do you know anyone in Edinburgh, Laura?' she asked a day or two later, when the young South African girl had recovered a little from the anaesthetic, and from the trauma of the accident. Kirsty was giving her a bed-bath.

Laura Barnard shook her head.

'None of us does,' she said. 'Margie and Jan and I were at university together, in Stellenbosch—that's near Cape Town. We've been on holiday, mostly on the continent. We—we were supposed to be going home next week, and we were determined to come to Scotland. Jan's grandparents came from further north, near Inverness, and we thought we'd see if there were any relatives still there. That's where we were heading. Jan feels awful about the accident, but it wasn't her fault; the other car just came out of a side-road.'

Laura's friends came to see her as soon as they could, but they were discharged just in time to fly to London, and then home to South Africa. After that, Laura was on her own. Sometimes at visiting time Kirsty would see a loneliness and a longing in Laura's blue eyes that caught at her heart.

Her own home was in Perth, so she had no family in Edinburgh, but in her years of nursing here at St Luke's she had made quite a few friends, and, after a little leaning here and there, she soon had a few visitors organised for Laura. The South African girl was a little shy, a little reserved, Kirsty found, but she obviously appreciated not being alone at visiting times.

One day, handing Laura a letter with a South African stamp, Kirsty said to her, 'Don't your folks want to come over, Laura, now that this has happened—just to make sure you're all right?'

Her own mother had come through to Edinburgh when she'd had flu, and again when she'd had laryngitis.

Laura's blue eyes were shadowed.

'My parents are both dead,' she said. 'There's only Mark and me—Mark is my brother; he's a doctor, and he's in private practice, so it wouldn't be easy for him to get away. But he's keeping in touch with Mr Martin, and he writes to me every week.'

'And when your cast comes off, and you're able to be mobile again?' Kirsty asked, concerned. 'Are you going to go straight back home?'

Laura turned away.

'I haven't really thought about that,' she said quickly. Too quickly, Kirsty found herself thinking. 'It—it's going to be very strange, getting out of this bed, moving around again.'

'You'll need physiotherapy, but of course you'll be able to have that at home,' Kirsty said. 'I bet you can't wait to get that cast off, and begin getting back to normal.'

Afterwards, she was to remember saying that. And she would look back on the weeks that Laura's leg was in the cast, in traction, reassuring herself that everything had been done as it should, that no aspect of Laura's care had been omitted.

She herself had checked for any signs of circulatory impairment, had watched for signs of excessive pressure. Laura's toes and foot had been examined for blanching, or cyanosis, or swelling.

There had been nothing, at any time, to give any warning that when the cast was removed, when the surgeon, and Sister Maclean, and Staff Nurse Cameron stood beside Laura's bed, they would see all the colour leave her face, and they would hear her say unsteadily, 'I can't move my legs. I can't move either of my legs!'

Kirsty saw the swift glance between the surgeon and Sister Maclean.

'You're just out of practice, Laura,' the surgeon said reassuringly. 'Let's not forget it's three months since your accident. Don't you worry, now; we'll have another look at you tomorrow, when your leg has got used to being free again.'

'What if I can't walk ever again?' Laura said, and Kirsty could hear the hysteria rising in her voice. 'What if—if——?'

Mr Martin patted her hand.

'We'll not have talk like that, lass,' he said firmly. 'I'll be phoning your brother tomorrow night, and I'm sure I'll be able to give him good news of you.'

But there was no change the next day. White and distressed, and her forehead damp, Laura eventually shook her head.

'I can't move my legs at all,' she said. 'What's wrong with me, Mr Martin?'

The orthopaedic specialist shook his head.

'I'm certain there's nothing wrong, Laura,' he said firmly. But Kirsty could see the concern in his eyes.

'We'll have a few tests done, just to make sure, but there's no reason why this shouldn't sort itself out, so don't upset yourself; just have patience.'

The next day, Laura was moved into a small private ward just off the big, sunny general ward.

'Mr Martin's orders,' Sister Maclean said briefly, when Kirsty came on duty after her morning off duty.

Kirsty never had been good at accepting that you didn't question orders from sisters.

'But why?' she said. 'It's much more cheerful for her in the general ward; she's often said herself how much she likes all the coming and going.'

Fortunately, the other nurses often told Kirsty, Sister Maclean liked what she called an enquiring mind, so she replied without more than a mild note of reproach, 'Mr Martin's decision, Staff.'

And then, relenting—just in time, Kirsty knew, as she opened her mouth to protest—sister added, 'Actually, it's Laura's brother's decision; he felt she should be in a private room, for the various tests that are going to be done. She's still on my floor, Staff, and still in my care. And yours. Now, you'd better check on Mrs Jones—thank goodness she's going home tomorrow!'

Thus dismissed, Kirsty had no option but to go, and to say no more. But not, she thought as she checked Mrs Jones's and the other gastric-resection patients' blood-pressure and respiratory-rates, and noted that the appendectomy patient had a return of peristaltic sounds, to feel anything but rising anger at Laura's brother, Dr Mark Barnard.

'Just who does he think he is?' she said to Pat Turner, the other staff nurse, when they met in the sluice-room. 'Sitting thousands of miles away, giving orders to us at St Luke's!'

Expertly, the other nurse re-stacked the bedpans.

'These juniors—I should make her come back and do the bedpans again.' And then, 'I gather he has some pull here,' Pat said, washing her hands. 'Our Mr Martin has a nephew who's just gone out to work for a year in a private hospital Laura's brother is on the board of.'

Kirsty sniffed. 'So he thinks he can call the shots, I suppose,' she returned, disliking the unknown Dr Mark Barnard even more.

There was no doubt that Laura was lonely stuck in her small room on her own, and she should just say so, Kirsty suggested to her later.

Colour flooded the younger girl's cheeks.

'Oh, I couldn't do that,' she said hastily. 'Not if Mark thinks it's best for me to be in a private room.'

Kirsty looked at her.

'You're what—twenty-two, Laura?' she pointed out. 'You're old enough to make up your own mind.'

'Mark has always looked after me,' Laura said. 'He's ten years older than me—I was only twelve when our folks died. No, Kirsty, I'd better stay here.'

Kirsty looked round, but fortunately Sister wasn't within hearing distance.

'We're not supposed to have patients calling us by our first names,' she reminded Laura. 'It isn't professional.'

She had to hurry off then, as there was a bell ringing imperiously in the general ward, and they were short-staffed, because of a widespread flu that was wreaking havoc with the medical staff.

And in the next few days, as more and more of the nursing staff reported sick, Kirsty and the few who were left were run off their feet. Sister Maclean herself had to give in, and Kirsty, torn between apprehension and pride, became acting sister, reporting to the sister on Medical on the next floor.

She was writing up reports one day, long after she should have been off duty, when the bell rang from Laura's room. She glanced into the general ward, but Pat and the junior were both busy, so she straightened her cap on her brown curls, and hurried along the corridor, knowing that Laura would ring only if it was absolutely necessary. But as she reached the door the bell ran again, loud and long.

'Sorry, Laura,' Kirsty said, pushing the door open. 'You know how it is——'

She stopped.

A tall, dark man stood with his finger still on the bell. His dark eyebrows were drawn together, and his lean brown face was taut.

'I'm afraid I don't know how it is, Staff Nurse,' he said brusquely. 'All I know is that my sister could have been in need of urgent attention, and it's taken you this long to get here.'

His sister? So this was Dr Mark Barnard, was it?

Kirsty drew herself to her full height—which she had always thought was adequate, at five feet six, but this man towered over her.

'I came as soon as the bell rang,' she returned coolly. 'Laura, what is it you want?'

Laura flushed.

'It wasn't me,' she said, obviously distressed. 'Mark has just arrived and he——'

'I want to speak to someone in charge,' the big, dark man said. 'Where is Sister?'

I do not like this man, Kirsty thought with certainty. I knew I wouldn't like him, and I don't.

She lifted her chin. 'Sister is ill,' she told him. 'I am in charge.'

His glance swept over her staff nurse badge dismissively.

'Then I'll talk to Mr Martin,' he said.

He turned away, and picked up Laura's chart from the foot of the bed. Kirsty opened her mouth to speak and at that moment Dr Mark Barnard lifted his head and looked at her. His eyes were very dark, in the brown of his face. Very dark, and—very angry.

Kirsty wasn't sure what she had been going to say, but she thought better of saying anything. She turned on her heel, and walked back to Sister's office, but her hands were shaking with sheer anger as she picked up the charts she had been working on.

But before she could start there was a peremptory knock on her door.

'Staff Nurse—Cameron,' Mark Barnard said, 'could you let Mr Martin know that I'm here?'

'I'll tell his secretary,' Kirsty replied, her voice, she hoped, cool and professional. 'He's operating today, of course. What would you like me to say?'

Dr Barnard told her what to say. She left a message with Mr Martin's secretary, telling him that Dr Barnard had arrived from South Africa, and would like to see him as soon as possible. Then she picked up her pen again, but Laura's brother didn't take the hint and go. He stood towering above her desk, looking down at her.

'I am not at all satisfied with my sister's treatment,' he said abruptly.

Kirsty put her pen down.

'I beg your pardon?' she said, unable to stop herself.

He ignored that.

'Were there any signs of circulatory impairment while her leg was in a cast?' he asked her. 'Is there any possibility that the cast could have damaged the peroneal nerve?'

'There have been no signs of circulatory impairment, Dr Barnard,' Kirsty replied evenly. 'Mr Martin has taken every possibility into account, and Laura has been seen by two other orthopaedic specialists and two neurologists. They all agree that there is no apparent physical reason for her paralysis.'

Mark Barnard's dark brows drew together.

'There is a new medical electronics test,' he said. 'It uses pulsed electro-magnetic fields to detect the pace of healing in fractures. Has that been done? If not, I want it done.'

Kirsty stood up.

'Then I suggest you talk to Mr Martin about it,' she replied. 'If you will excuse me, Dr Barnard, I should have been off duty an hour ago.'

What an arrogant, insufferable man, she thought as she drew her cloak around her—for even in the covered walkway that connected the hospital and the nurses' home the chill of early December in Edinburgh managed to creep through. And then she thought, with only a little apprehension, But of course I should have been much more polite. Yes, Dr Barnard. No, Dr Barnard. Anything you say, Dr Barnard.

Anyway, she reminded herself as she slid gratefully into a hot bath some fifteen minutes later, he'll only be around for a few days, and then I suppose he'll whisk Laura back to South Africa. But he'll probably make his presence felt, well and truly, until then.

Which, as it turned out, was true. But not entirely as Kirsty had expected. There was certainly a considerable coming and going of specialists, there were conferences of very senior medical teams, there was the frequent use of the phone in Sister's office, and there was some disruption of normal routine. Although, she had to admit, Dr Barnard didn't actually seem to expect her to drop all her ward responsibilities; he did seem to realise that she was busy, and that they were short-staffed. No, she had expected all that. What she hadn't expected was the devastating effect of this big South African doctor on the rest of the staff.

'His eyes!' Pat breathed into her coffee in the duty-room one morning. 'Have you ever seen eyes so brooding, so—sort of sombre? Heathcliff eyes, I call them.'

'He is all man,' one junior agreed dreamily. 'Have you seen how brown his hands and his wrists are? I bet he's brown all over—well, pretty nearly! All that South African sunshine.'

'He certainly is all man,' the other junior agreed. 'I just love it when he talks in that velvet voice; I love the different way he says things.'

Kirsty set down her own coffee-mug with a bang that almost spilled the coffee in it.

'Och, you're all daft,' she said, exasperated. 'The

man is nothing special, as men go; I wouldn't be wasting my time on him. He's not even what you would call really good-looking, and him always with such a bad-tempered expression on his face! Not to mention thinking women should just jump when he snaps his fingers.' That, she knew, wasn't really fair, but she didn't feel like being fair.

She stood up, and drained her coffee.

'There's plenty work to be done,' she said briskly, trying to sound as much like Sister Maclean as possible. 'I'm going back to the office.'

At the door, she turned.

'All man, indeed,' she said.

She closed the duty-room door behind her, and almost bumped into a tall figure.

'Ah—Staff Nurse Cameron,' Dr Mark Barnard said smoothly. 'I was looking for you.'

He couldn't have heard, he couldn't possibly, Kirsty told herself as she looked up at him. But somehow there was something in his face that told her that he just might have. Something in his eyes. Heathcliff eyes, Pat had said.

She dismissed that thought.

'I do have a short coffee-break at this time,' she said, knowing she sounded defensive, and annoyed at herself for that.

He acknowledged that with a slight nod.

'I just wanted to tell you that the result of that test shows that there is complete healing in the fracture. So there is no reason there for this paralysis.'

Little as she liked the man, Kirsty could see how worried he was.

'Are you satisfied with the other tests that have been done, Dr Barnard?' she asked him as they went into the office.

'I have to be,' he said after a moment. 'There's only one report still to come in, and I don't suppose it will tell us anything we don't already know.'

Kirsty hesitated.

'Maybe it will just take time, and physiotherapy,' she suggested. 'And maybe being back at home will help Laura, too.'

For there is nothing more that can be done for her here, she thought, and she could see that the big man knew what she was thinking. Knew, and perhaps wasn't prepared, or able, to accept that.

The cool hostility was back in his eyes as he looked down at her, and her momentary sympathy for him evaporated.

'I'm not giving up yet,' he said brusquely.

He turned on his heel and walked away down the corridor, towards his sister's room.

It's not a question of giving up, Kirsty thought. But you are not doing Laura any good by putting her through test after test. She is losing hope; she's getting more and more depressed and worried.

The next day, Mr Martin, the neurologist and Mark Barnard were in Laura's room for a long time. Too long, Kirsty thought darkly, seeing them eventually leave, and knowing, even before she went along to Laura's room, how she would find the girl.

There was no need to ask if the final tests had shown anything new. Laura's white face, the shadows under her blue eyes, told her that even before Laura shook her head.

'No medical or surgical or neurological reason,' she said a little shakily. 'So why can't I walk, Kirsty?'

'It doesn't look as if there's any answer to that, Laura,' Kirsty said. 'I think myself that you need to forget about any more tests, and try just to take things as they come, a wee while at a time.'

She could see that Laura was close to tears.

'But I don't know what I'll do with my nurses,' she said, trying to cheer her patient up a little, 'when you take your brother away, for every one of them thinks he's the cat's whiskers.'

A faint smile touched the corner of Laura's mouth, and Kirsty tried a little harder.

'As for me,' she said, 'I'm still faithful to Robert Redford.'

'Isn't he a bit old for you?' Laura asked, and the smile began to grow.

'Maybe a wee bit,' Kirsty admitted. 'But then again, what's a few years with a man like him?'

This time, Laura laughed aloud, and Kirsty, delighted, laughed too, dislodging her cap from her brown curls. She was still laughing as she pinned it back in place again. At that moment, Mark Barnard walked in.

'I was just going, Dr Barnard,' Kirsty said hastily, catching sight of the dismay in her hazel eyes, of her flushed cheeks, of her completely unprofessional appearance, in Laura's mirror.

Mark Barnard followed her out into the corridor.

'I'm glad you don't find my sister's condition too depressing, Staff,' he said coldly.

'That isn't fair, Dr Barnard,' Kirsty replied, stung. 'I was only trying to cheer Laura up a bit!'

Back in Sister's office, she told herself again how much she disliked this man, how little it mattered to her what he thought of her. But it hurt, all the same, she had to admit that.

When the bell from Laura's room rang, her heart sank. But it had to be answered. She took a deep breath, and went along.

Mark Barnard was looking out of the window at the sleety December rain falling steadily.

'I am making arrangements to take Laura home, Nurse Cameron,' he said, without turning round.

'I'm sure that's the best thing for her, Dr Barnard,' Kirsty agreed primly.

'There is only one thing.'

He turned round, his dark brows drawn together.

'Laura has this foolish idea that she would like you to give up your job here and come with us. She will need help and attention for a while, of course.' His lean face was set in forbidding lines. 'I have told her that I am quite certain you couldn't consider it.'

Perhaps it was the way he said it, perhaps it was the rain and the sleet of a December day in Edinburgh, perhaps it was the way Laura was looking at her, the way she was waiting.

Whatever the reason, Kirsty lifted her chin, looked straight at Dr Mark Barnard and said, clearly, 'I don't know about that, Dr Barnard. I'd certainly like to think about it.'

CHAPTER TWO

KIRSTY didn't have to think about her decision for long.

She'd always had this restless sort of feeling, this desire to do something different, something exciting, and now the chance was being handed to her on a plate, and there was nothing to stop her saying yes, and going to South Africa as Laura's nurse. There was no one special in her love-life, for although she was never short of dates or social life there hadn't been anyone she had felt committed to.

Sister Maclean was back at work, as were most of the staff who had been down with flu, and Kirsty herself had enough holiday due to her to let her hand in her notice and leave almost right away.

'Do you really want me to come with you?' she asked Laura the next day.

Laura's blue eyes were steady.

'I don't think I can face it without you,' she said simply. She was in a wheelchair now, sitting beside the window. 'To go back, like this—please say you'll come with me, Kirsty.'

Kirsty took a deep breath.

'I'll come.'

But the dismay in Mark Barnard's dark eyes when she said the same to him, later that day, was almost enough to make her change her mind. Almost, but not quite.

'You're quite sure, Nurse Cameron?' he said. 'I don't want to make all the preparations, book tickets, get everything fixed up, and then have you getting cold feet and changing your mind.'

'I'm not in the habit of changing my mind after I give my word, Dr Barnard,' Kirsty said evenly.

'There won't be much of a social life; we live on a

farm between Cape Town and Stellenbosch, and there are no bright lights, no buses to take you anywhere exciting,' the big doctor said.

Kirsty drew herself up, conscious once again of just how big this man was. Big, and forbidding.

'I don't think you know me well enough to think that I would need bright lights, Dr Barnard,' she returned.

His dark eyebrows rose.

'Just a country girl at heart?' he asked sardonically.

Kirsty forced herself to remain silent, and after a moment Mark Barnard shrugged.

'Right,' he said, 'I'll go ahead and book our flight.'

He bent down and kissed Laura's cheek, his big brown hand resting on her slight shoulder.

'I've got a lot to do—see you this evening.'

When he had gone, Laura looked up at Kirsty.

'I'm sorry, Kirsty,' she said, all too clearly embarrassed. 'Mark doesn't mean to be rude.'

I'm not so sure about that, Kirsty thought, but I'm darned if I'm going to let it bother me!

'Don't worry, Laura,' she said. 'I can't say we've taken to each other—that's pretty obvious—but I'm sure your brother and I are quite capable of putting up with each other.'

Or, she thought, of keeping well out of each other's way, and perhaps that will be the best thing.

The reaction among the rest of the nurses on Women's Surgical was, she thought, fairly predictable.

'Going to South Africa, with Dr Mark Barnard?' Pat said, her voice hushed.

'No, with Laura, as her nurse,' Kirsty returned. 'Look, maybe she'll get back the use of her legs soon, and then I won't be there for long, but it's a chance to see a bit more of the world.'

'What I'd like,' Pat said, 'is a chance to see more of Mark Barnard. Much more of him.'

She giggled, and the junior giggled too.

'Don't be crude,' Kirsty said coldly. And then, in spite of herself, she giggled too.

The last days in Scotland flew past. Mark arranged for Laura to spend a week at a convalescent home outside Edinburgh while he attended a medical conference at the university. Kirsty managed to have a few days at home before leaving, grateful for her family's matter-of-fact reaction to her news.

Her mother said philosophically that Scots folk had always had it in their blood to settle in foreign lands. Her father said that was no wonder—they would do anything to get away from Scottish weather. Her young brother said hopefully that maybe his school would decide to send a cricket team out, and her grandmother remembered that a second cousin had gone to settle in Johannesburg thirty years ago. Kirsty pointed out that she would be near Cape Town, and Johannesburg was as far away as Rome.

But in spite of all that she couldn't help feeling a catch in her throat as the plane took off, and the clouds hid Edinburgh from her sight.

'No regrets?' Mark Barnard said.

That wouldn't be sympathy in his voice surely? Kirsty told herself. She lifted her chin.

'None at all,' she assured him, not entirely truthfully, and she turned to Laura to ask her if she was comfortable.

The short flight to London wasn't a problem, but the long, thirteen-hour flight to Cape Town was far from easy. They had been given seats as close to the toilets as possible, and Kirsty, with the help of the air hostess, took Laura there when it was necessary, and tried to make her as comfortable as possible during the long hours in the air. They were flying club class, and the extra space made a big difference, but it was still difficult and trying for Laura, Kirsty thought, looking at the younger girl's white face, at the shadows under her eyes.

Laura did sleep, for a few hours, and once she was sure that her patient was as comfortable as possible, and soundly asleep, Kirsty felt her own eyelids becom-

ing heavy. On the other side of her, Mark Barnard
had turned his small light on, although the rest of the
huge cabin was in darkness, and he was studying some
papers. Probably from the conference, Kirsty thought
drowsily, giving up the effort to keep her eyes open.

She woke with a start, to find her head resting
comfortably on Mark Barnard's shoulder. On the point
of moving away, horrified, she realised that he was
asleep too, his dark head resting against hers. She
didn't know how long she sat there, embarrassed,
wondering what on earth she would do or say when
he woke and at the same time unwilling to move in
case he did wake.

When he did, he stretched, and for a moment his
dark eyes looked right into hers. He needed a shave,
she found herself thinking as the roughness of his chin
touched her cheek with an intimacy that was decidedly
disturbing, even if accidental.

'You look different out of uniform, Nurse Cameron,'
he said, and Kirsty wasn't sure whether it was surprise
or amusement in his voice. That, and a sort of sleepy
warmth. Defensively, she tried to tidy her hair, knowing it must be tousled and unruly after the restless
night, and conscious, too, that in jeans and a T-shirt
she must indeed look different.

What was it the girls at the hospital had said about
Mark Barnard?

'He's all man'.

Ridiculous, she thought, to remember that now.
Except that it was difficult not to, when the confines
of the plane forced her to be so close to him.

'You can't call her Nurse Cameron, Mark,' Laura
said sleepily, and Kirsty turned to her in relief.

Mark Barnard stood up.

'I'm going along to wash and shave,' he said. And
then, 'No, I don't suppose I can. It's Kirsty, isn't it?'

He was completely awake now, and the sleepy
warmth had gone from his voice. If it had ever been
there at all, Kirsty thought.

'I've never seen dawn from a plane,' she said to
Laura as the air hostess handed them glasses of
orange juice.

'Wait till you see dawn in the bushveld,' Laura told
her. 'And sunset over the Cape mountains.'

Kirsty looked at her.

'You are glad to be going home, Laura?' she asked
carefully, because sometimes there had been something—a shadow on Laura's face, a hesitation in her
voice—that had made her wonder.

Even now, it was a moment before Laura replied.

'Yes, of course I am.' And then, again, 'Yes, I'm
glad to be going home, Kirsty.'

And there was no doubt about the delight on her
face at the first sight of Table Mountain from the plane.
And later, the formalities over, and their luggage
packed into a Land Rover driven by one of the men
from the farm, as they headed away from the incredible
sight of Table Mountain rising sheer into the blue sky,
towards the distant range of mountains, blue and hazy,
Laura leaned forward, obviously happy to recognise
familiar places.

And yet—and yet—there had been that momentary
hesitation, that shadow in her eyes.

Och, away with you, Kirsty told herself severely,
echoing her grandmother's usual reprimand. Of course
the girl feels strange about coming back in a wheelchair, when she left here on her own two feet. It would
get anyone down.

Afterwards, she thought that she would never forget
her first sight of Bloemenkloof, the old house, gleam-
ing white in the sunshine, with the gables, and the
thatched roof, set among the vineyards, with the rugged blue mountains behind it. And the long veranda
running the length of the house, with green vines and
purple bougainvillaea intertwined to give it shade, and,
as she later found, coolness.

'That veranda!' she said as she opened the door of
the Land Rover.

'We call it a *stoep* here,' Mark Barnard told her.

For a moment, she thought he was going to help
her down from the high step, but he turned away as
the big front door of the house opened and a large
black woman came hurrying down. She ignored Mark,
Kirsty and the driver of the Land Rover.

'About time they brought you home, Laura,' she
said sternly. Then she turned to Mark. 'You get this
girl into her room, now, Mark, she looks worn out.'

'I'll get her in right away, Sarah,' Mark Barnard said
meekly and obediently.

Kirsty looked at him, unable to hide her astonish-
ment, as Sarah hurried back up the wide steps.

'Sarah has pretty much brought us up,' Mark said
quietly. 'She was my nanny, and then Laura's.'

He lifted his sister out of the Land Rover, and held
her while the man who had driven them got the
wheelchair out.

'And afterwards,' Laura said, her fair head resting
against him, 'when when Mum and Dad were killed
in the plane crash, we couldn't have managed without
Sarah, could we, Mark?'

'No, we couldn't,' the big doctor agreed. 'And we
still couldn't manage without her, and well she
knows it!'

Gently, carefully, he put Laura in the wheelchair,
and Kirsty, watching, saw his knuckles become white
as he began to push it towards the house.

'Mind giving me a hand to lift this up?' he asked
the driver, his voice light, casual. And then, with an
effort that Kirsty thought perhaps she was the only
one who saw, he smiled, and when the wheelchair was
lifted up the wide steps he said that they'd have to
have a ramp for the chair; he hadn't thought of it
until now.

No wonder he's sometimes bad-tempered and arrogant, with the worry of it all, Kirsty thought, a little
ashamed of her own hostility towards him. How would
I be feeling if this were my brother, and him unable

to walk, and no one able to say why? And with that thought, that understanding, she told herself that she should be able to feel more generous towards this man.

The house was in the shape of an H, and Laura's room opened out into a sheltered paved courtyard. It was a large and sunny room, and Kirsty saw, with a swift glance, that it would be an easy room for her to manage in, nursing Laura—for as long as nursing was needed. And maybe that will only be for a wee while, she told herself, determined that she was going to be positive about the girl in her care.

Swiftly, professionally, she got Laura freshened and changed.

'I got your bed ready, Laura,' Sarah said, coming in with a tray of tea, and some sandwiches.

Laura's soft mouth tightened.

'I'm not going to bed, Sarah,' she said. And then, appealing to Kirsty, 'I'm not an invalid, am I, Kirsty? I just—I just——' Her voice faltered.

Kirsty waited for a moment, knowing it would be better if Laura would say the words herself. But she quickly realised that right now she would have to be the one to say them.

'You just can't walk, for the moment,' she said steadily. 'But there's no reason why you won't be able to pretty soon.' She glanced around the room.

'I certainly don't think you should go to bed, Laura,' she said briskly. 'But a wee while lying down on that nice couch at the door wouldn't be a bad idea. Right, let's get you settled.' Silently, and with some suspicion, she was sure, Sarah helped her.

'Now we'll have a nice cup of tea. Thanks, Sarah, I certainly need this, and I'm sure you do, Laura—and you can just sit and look out, and get the fresh air at the same time.'

Gratefully, Laura took the cup of tea and, after a moment's hesitation, a sandwich. Sarah nodded, satisfied.

'Dr Barnard said you should have the room next to

Laura, Nurse,' she said formally. 'There's a bathroom in between the two.'

Kirsty, on the point of suggesting cheerfully that Sarah should call her Kirsty, had a sudden realisation that any change in formality would have to come from Sarah herself. So, with the same meekness that Mark Barnard had shown, she allowed herself to be taken through to the room that was to be hers.

It was a pretty room—smaller than Laura's, but still spacious, and also with a door that opened on to the courtyard. There was a big mirror, framed in a golden wood that was unfamiliar to Kirsty, with a big wooden chest of the same wood at the foot of the bed. Kirsty peered at herself in the mirror critically. Tired, and a wee bit washed-out-looking, she told herself. Peely-wally was the word Granny would use. And her T-shirt and jeans were crumpled from the long journey.

The girl in the mirror looked back at her solemnly. And then the hazel eyes crinkled, and the mouth that Kirsty always thought could have been smaller began to smile.

Och, a bath and a change of clothes and I'll be fine, she told herself.

And fine she was, half an hour later, her hair still damp, and curling around her face, and wearing a pink cotton dress—bought in Marks & Spencer last summer and hardly worn. She looked ruefully at her bare legs, and her feet in sandals, and decided that she would have to get a bit of a tan.

Laura had fallen asleep, her fair head resting back against the cushion, and Kirsty moved her slightly, to make her more comfortable, and then went outside, with the door open so that she could check on Laura.

Just outside, she stopped.

Mark Barnard was sitting at the white wicker table, drinking tea, his dark head bent over a pile of letters.

'Oh, Dr Barnard, I didn't know you were there,' Kirsty said awkwardly, and annoyed at herself for feeling that.

'No? Well, I am,' he said fairly pleasantly, without looking up. 'Sit down and pour yourself some tea—I'm catching up on post.'

'Thanks, but I've had some,' Kirsty replied.

'Have some more, then; it's always a good idea after a long flight,' the doctor said absently.

He looked up. He didn't say anything, but his dark eyes widened as he looked at her. And Kirsty, to her horror, felt her cheeks grow warm under his gaze. I knew this dress was too short, she thought. And a wee bit low at the neck.

Still Mark Barnard said nothing, and Kirsty felt so uncomfortable that she had to speak.

'Maybe you would rather I wore uniform, Dr Barnard,' she said, more abruptly than she had meant to. 'I do have uniforms with me, but Laura said I wouldn't need to—but if you think it would be more suitable, then of course I can change.'

The doctor shook his head.

'No, of course not. I was just—surprised, that's all.'

Surprised at what? Kirsty wondered, but she didn't have the courage to ask. Realising that she was thirsty, she poured some tea for herself.

'The swimming-pool is at the back,' Mark said. 'Swim any time you feel like it—if you haven't brought a costume, I'm sure Laura can lend you one.' His dark eyes moved over her thoughtfully. Was that amusement Kirsty was seeing? 'Although I think Laura's bathing costumes might be a little small for you.'

If it was possible, Kirsty felt her cheeks grow even warmer.

'Laura is a bit thinner than me,' she agreed, hoping her voice was steady. 'But I have brought a costume, and thank you, I would like to swim.'

He is different at home, she thought, warmer, more casual, and somehow he doesn't seem as hostile towards me as he was in Edinburgh.

As if to confirm this, Mark Barnard smiled. And he did, Kirsty realised, have a very nice smile.

Taken aback by her own thoughts, because she had
been so certain that her feelings of dislike for this man
were very clear, she hastily changed the subject.

'The flowers are beautiful,' she said quickly. 'What
is that white bush with the lovely smell?'

'Frangipani,' Mark Barnard told her. 'And that one
there, with the flowers in three different colours, has
a lovely smell too. It's called Yesterday, Today and
Tomorrow. We have a rose garden beside the pool—if
you're interested in gardens, you'll like that.'

'I do like roses,' Kirsty said. 'But we have roses at
home; it's these different ones I'm more interested in,
Dr Barnard.'

'What's this "Dr Barnard" business?' he said. 'I
thought Laura gave us our orders on that—Kirsty.'

Before she could reply, he looked at his watch, and
stood up.

'I'm late,' he said. 'See you at dinner.'

He walked across the courtyard, and through a
door at the far side. Kirsty finished her tea, thinking
with some surprise that maybe the girls on Women's
Surgical had been right—maybe Mark Barnard was
nicer than she had given him credit for.

Laura woke soon after that, looking considerably
more rested. Kirsty helped her into the wheelchair,
and pushed her out to the courtyard.

'It's still a lovely day, Laura,' she said. 'Wouldn't
you like me to take you for a wee walk around the
garden? Your brother was saying you have a nice rose
garden; we could have a look at that.'

Laura turned away, but not before Kirsty had seen
the shadow on her face.

'No, I—I don't want to do that, Kirsty,' she said
quickly. 'I'm quite happy to stay here for a bit.'

Kirsty didn't want to insist, but she knew that the
longer Laura put off being seen in her wheelchair, here
in her own home, the harder it would be. But today
was perhaps too soon; perhaps it was better left for
the moment.

The heat of the day had gone a little, and in the cooler air the fragrance of the flowering bushes was even stronger. Mark had said he'd see them at dinner, Kirsty told Laura, and Laura said that of course he would have a lot to do, after being away.

'Do we have to change?' Kirsty asked doubtfully, the word 'dinner' bothering her, but Laura shook her head and said it would only be themselves.

Just before seven, Kirsty pushed the wheelchair along the wide, wooden-floored corridor to the dining-room, just behind the big room at the entrance.

'This is the *agterkamer*, and the one you come into is the *voorkamer*,' Laura told her casually. And when Kirsty asked she said that *voorkamer* meant the room in front and *agterkamer* the room behind.

'Most of the Cape Dutch houses are planned that way,' she said. 'This one was built in 1820, so it isn't one of the oldest. Our family has only had it for about a hundred years, so——'

She stopped.

A young man, tall, sun-bronzed, his fair hair bleached golden by the sun, strode through the door, his hands held out.

'Laura, love,' he said, going straight to the girl in the wheelchair. 'I've missed you—I'm glad you're home.'

He bent and kissed her. He would, Kirsty saw, have kissed her mouth, but Laura moved, so that his lips met her cheek.

'Simon,' Laura said quickly, 'this is Kirsty Cameron; she's looking after me. Kirsty, Simon is our cousin—well, second cousin, but he's a Barnard too—he manages the farm, and makes our wine.'

The fair-haired young man turned to Kirsty. His eyes were very blue in the brown of his face, and the admiration in them was undisguised.

'Well, now,' he said softly, and he took both Kirsty's hands in his, 'why didn't anyone tell me about you, Kirsty Cameron?'

Kirsty wanted to free her hands, but they were

imprisoned by Simon Barnard as his blue eyes smiled down at her.

'Ah, Simon, I see you've met Laura's nurse,' Mark said, his voice cool.

Kirsty managed to free her hands as Simon turned towards the man in the doorway.

And that, she thought, puts me well and truly in my place. Laura's nurse.

Whatever warmth and welcome there had been in the doctor's lean brown face as they'd sat together that afternoon had gone. All his earlier hostility was there, and more, Kirsty realised, dismayed. Dismayed, and annoyed with herself for feeling that way.

For there was no reason at all for her to care what this man thought of her, she reminded herself. She'd been right in her earlier assessment of him—arrogant, sure of himself.

The less you and I have to do with each other the better, Dr Mark Barnard, she told herself. That's obviously the way you want it, and it's certainly the way I want it!

CHAPTER THREE

BUT, in spite of this certainty that she didn't want to see any more of Mark Barnard than she had to, Kirsty was a little taken aback to find, the next morning, when she took Laura through for breakfast, that he had already gone.

'He has to get back to work; his locum can't fill in any longer,' Laura explained. 'And we're twenty minutes out of Stellenbosch, where his consulting-rooms are, so he has to leave early.'

Sarah, who had told them Mark had gone—or rather 'the doctor' had gone—turned from putting Mark's dirty dishes on a tray, and said to Laura, 'How you like your egg today, Laura?'

'I won't have any egg, thanks, Sarah, just fruit and toast,' Laura said.

Sarah folded her arms. 'And why not?' she demanded, looking down at Laura.

'People shouldn't eat egg every day; it's bad for your cholesterol,' Laura replied.

'You eat your egg yesterday?' Sarah asked.

'Er—well, no, I didn't,' Laura admitted.

'Then how you like it today?' Sarah said implacably.

'Poached, thank you, Sarah,' Laura said meekly, after a moment.

Sarah turned to Kirsty. 'And you, Nurse?' she asked, in a voice that Kirsty wouldn't have dared to argue with.

'Poached too, thank you,' Kirsty said.

There was fruit set out on a huge old sideboard, and when Sarah had gone Laura manoeuvred her wheel-chair, a little awkwardly, over to it. Kirsty watched her, ready to help if necessary, but knowing that the more Laura did for herself, and the more independent

30

she became, the better. But the sideboard was high,
and the slice of sweet melon Laura had managed to
put on a plate slipped off. Laura's fair skin flushed,
and she bit her lip. 'I thought I could manage,' she
said apologetically.

'Don't worry,' Kirsty told her, and she picked up
the fruit from the floor, set it aside, and put sweet
melon on two plates. 'I like this room,' she said,
looking around, and giving Laura a chance to
recover. 'Your dining-room—what did you call it?
The *agterkamer*?—it's a beautiful room, but a bit for-
mal; I prefer this smaller one.'

The small room was situated off the big dining-room,
and the morning sunlight streamed in. The window-
frames, Kirsty saw, were made of the same golden
wood that she had admired in her bedroom, and she
asked Laura about it.

'It's yellowwood,' Laura told her. 'Most of it comes
from the forests around Knysna, up the coast. There's
a lot of it used in old Cape Dutch houses.'

'I love the chest,' Kirsty said, going back for some
more sweet melon.

'It's a *kist*,' Laura told her.

'A *kist*?' Kirsty repeated, surprised. 'But that's a
Scottish word for a chest!'

'It comes from old Dutch with us, but you'll feel
quite at home with it, then,' Laura said, laughing.

Sarah, coming into the room with the eggs, and
some toast, looked from Laura to Kirsty, and Kirsty
thought that it was approval she saw in the older
woman's face.

A little later, when Laura was telephoning Jan, one
of the girls who had been with her when the accident
happened, Kirsty went to look for Sarah.

'I wonder, Sarah,' she said carefully, 'whether you
might be able to set the fruit out on a lower table for
breakfast?'

Sarah's face was impassive, and she said nothing.

'It's just that Laura can't reach it,' Kirsty went on,

'and it really would be better for her to be able to do things for herself.'

Her heart sank as Sarah still said nothing. She's always looked after Laura, she reminded herself; she probably thinks I should do all I can for her, especially since it's what I'm paid for, as her nurse.

She tried again.

'It isn't that I mind doing things for her,' she said, 'but while she's in the wheelchair the more independent she can be the better.'

Still silence.

And then, like the sun breaking through clouds, Sarah smiled.

'You're right, Nurse,' she said. 'We got a lower table; Laura will be able to reach that. I see to it.' She turned to go back to the kitchen, but at the door she turned. 'It's good that you make Laura laugh,' she said.

But Laura looked far from laughter, Kirsty thought, when she went into the big sunny room and found Laura's wheelchair beside the small table where the phone was. Laura's hand was still on the replaced phone.

'Did you get your friend?' Kirsty asked.

Laura nodded.

'Yes, thank you,' she said politely. 'She's coming out to see me tomorrow.'

'That's nice,' Kirsty replied. And then, sitting down beside the younger girl, she said gently, 'Anything I can help with, Laura?'

Laura bit her lip.

'It's just—oh, it's silly of me, but Jan has got a job, and she's so excited about starting work, and——'

She looked down at her useless legs.

'I've never asked you what you do, Laura,' Kirsty said. In some ways, it might be easier, and kinder, to talk about something else, not to let Laura dwell on this, but Kirsty had always believed in facing up to things, and her instinctive feeling was that it would be better for Laura to do the same.

Laura managed to smile, but it wasn't a smile that reached her eyes.

'I did teacher training,' she said. 'I want to go on and do remedial teaching, but—but Mark doesn't think it's a good idea.'

'Mark doesn't think it's a good idea?' Kirsty repeated, astounded and with rising anger. 'Laura, you're old enough to know what you want to do.'

Laura's fair face flushed.

'Mark thinks I would find it very demanding emotionally,' she said, her voice low.

'You probably would,' Kirsty agreed levelly. 'But that's no reason not to go ahead and do it.' And then, unable to restrain herself, she burst out, 'For heaven's sake, Laura, he's got no right to stop you doing what you want to!'

'He won't stop me if I really want to,' Laura said quietly. 'That was one of the things I was supposed to be thinking about, on our overseas holiday. Of course, now there isn't any question of it.'

'Laura,' Kirsty said sternly.

With difficulty, Laura smiled.

'I mean at the moment,' she said.

But—one of the things? Kirsty wondered about that, but just then there was a whining and a scratching at the door.

'It's Rufus!' Laura said, her face lighting up. 'Let him in, please, Kirsty.'

Rufus was a handsome red setter, his red-gold coat glossy. He came bounding in, right over to Laura's wheelchair. Laura fondled the silky head, and the big dog whined with pleasure.

'Why weren't you here yesterday, boy?' she said to him.

Sarah, coming in just then, had the answer to that.

'I told Simon to keep Rufus down at his house; I thought maybe he jump too much, but he must have got out, and come right here. Now you be careful, dog, in this room!'

Rufus, unrepentant, wagged his plumed tail, and then looked hopefully up at Laura.

'He wants to go out,' Sarah said unneccessarily.

Kirsty saw Laura's hand become still on the dog's head. And then Laura looked at her, her blue eyes meeting Kirsty's.

'Then let's take him out,' she said steadily. 'Can you get someone to lift the wheelchair down the steps, Sarah?'

'No need,' Sarah said gruffly. 'We got a ramp for the chair; Mark got it done right away.'

The day was hot and still, and the mountains were blue and hazy. Kirsty pushed the wheelchair along a wide dirt road that led through the vineyards. There were people working at the far end of one of them, and she recognised Simon Barnard's sun-bleached head. He waved to them, his arm brown against the deep blue of his short-sleeved shirt.

The dog ran ahead of them at first, bounding eagerly along the path, but after a while he came back and walked beside them.

They passed more groups of farm workers, some weeding the vineyards, others tying up shoots of trel- lised vines. Each time, the men and women who were working straightened up and waved to the girls. Laura, from her wheelchair, waved back, and so did Kirsty.

And that, Kirsty thought, as they headed for the house again, was at least a start. Looking at the situ- ation positively, since there was no medical reason for Laura being unable to walk, perhaps she would regain the use of her legs very soon, and then there would be no need for her to face people in a wheelchair. But you had to be realistic, and surely it was better to accept things as they were right now.

There was a dark blue German car drawn up at the steps of the house.

'Mark's home,' Laura said, obviously pleased. 'He doesn't usually come home at lunchtime.'

Lunch was set out in the same small room, an informal lunch of cold chicken and salad. The doctor was already eating when Kirsty and Laura went in.

'You look better, Laura,' he said, coming over to them. 'You've got some colour in your cheeks.'

'We've been for a walk,' Laura told him. 'We took Rufus out through the fields, almost to the river.'

'Good,' Mark said.

Looking at the two of them, brother and sister, Kirsty had to admit that whatever her own reservations about this man, both as a man and as Laura's brother, there was a real warm affection between them. Not that that gave Mark Barnard the right to manage Laura's life, she reminded herself, but it was something that she should keep reminding herself of.

And she had to do that, very strongly, when Mark, standing up to finish the cup of coffee he was drinking, told Laura he was arranging for her to have more tests done.

'I want them done as soon as possible,' he said. 'I'm leaning on Bill Brown, so if he can fix anything up we'll get you through to Cape Town tomorrow. If I can't get away, Simon can take you. Oh, and I'm getting a physiotherapist fixed up; I want her here to see you tomorrow or the next day, depending on when Bill Brown can see you.'

All the colour had left Laura's cheeks.

'Oh, Mark, do I have to have more tests?' she asked, not quite steadily. 'I thought Mr Martin in Edinburgh said everything possible had been checked.'

Mark put his coffee-cup down on the table.

'I want Bill Brown to do his own tests,' he said decisively. 'Leave it to me, Laura.' He looked at his watch, bent and kissed Laura's cheek. 'Time I was off,' he said. 'See you tonight.'

And that, I suppose, was meant for me too, Kirsty told herself as he hurried out, with a nod in her direction.

There was a small sound from Laura. She wasn't crying, but she was close to it, Kirsty saw.

'Surely I don't need any more tests done?' Laura
said unsteadily. 'I don't need anyone else to tell me
there's no medical reason why I can't walk? It's—it's
very depressing; I almost wish they'd find out something definite. I don't mind the physiotherapist. Mr
Martin said I'd need that; he said it would keep the
muscles in my legs in good order. But I don't want
more tests done.'

Laura's distress was all Kirsty needed to confirm her
own thoughts. With a quick word to Laura, she hurried
out after the doctor. He was just opening his car door.

'Mark, it really bothers Laura, having more tests
done,' she said breathlessly. 'Surely there isn't any
need for that, when she had everything possible done
in Edinburgh? Even that special electro-magnetic one
to detect the pace of healing.'

Mark's dark eyebrows drew together forbiddingly.

'You must allow me to know what's best for Laura,'
he said, his voice dripping ice.

She didn't give herself time to think.

'Are you so sure you know what's best for her?' she
said hotly.

'Of course I'm sure,' the doctor replied, his voice
impatient as well as icy now.

But Kirsty was determined that she wasn't giving up
that easily.

'You have all the reports from Edinburgh,' she said.
'Could you not just let this man see them, check their
findings?'

He looked down at her, unsmiling, and slowly some
of Kirsty's confidence left her.

'I'm sorry,' she said reluctantly. 'It's just—I can see
how it upsets Laura, the thought of having more tests
done, more people telling her there's no medical
reason why she can't walk.'

Mark was very close to her. So close that she could
see a small muscle move in his cheek. He was, she
realised, very angry with her.

'Do you think,' he said, 'that I could live with myself

if I had not done everything possible, if I had not moved heaven and earth, to get my sister out of that damned wheelchair?'

Without another word, he got into the car, slammed the door, and drove off.

Just walking away from Kirsty Cameron didn't mean that he could forget what she had said, Mark found as he drove to his surgery.

Damned girl, he told himself angrily. She doesn't know Laura as I do—of course I know what's best.

But by the time he had seen his first three patients—a four-year-old boy with query asthma, an old lady with arthritis, and a student he had been seeing fairly regularly with a recurring glandular fever, Kirsty Cameron had been relegated to the back of his mind.

His next patient, Ken Harris, was a local banker Mark had known for years. A few months ago, he had had to confirm his diagnosis of multiple sclerosis. Ken's wife, Greta, was with him on this visit, and when Mark had finished his examination, she said, 'I just want to know, Mark, if there isn't anything more we can do. I take Ken to the phsyiotherapist once a week, but his legs aren't getting any stronger.'

'No, but we're keeping the muscle tone from deteriorating any further, Greta,' Mark said.

He looked at the man across from him. Multiple sclerosis. A chronic, progressive disease of the central nervous system. Already Ken had gone through the early stages—visual disturbances, vertigo, loss of muscle tone.

'You're in remission now, Ken,' he said. 'And that's good.'

'But for how long?' Greta asked unsteadily.

'I can't say,' Mark told her. And then, gently, 'You know that, Greta; we've talked about it before.'

Now it was Ken who spoke.

'And when the remission ends?' he asked levelly. 'A wheelchair?'

'Probably, at a later stage,' Mark replied, for he knew this man needed the truth. 'And we'll have you on a high dosage of ACTH—that could help. We'll step up the phsyiotherapy, too.'

He walked to the door with them, Ken leaning heavily on his stick.

'Any change, any time, ring me,' he said.

'Thanks, Mark,' Ken said, his voice steady. 'See you.'

They're strong, they'll take it, Mark thought as he went back to his desk. But they'll need every bit of that strength.

For a moment, his thoughts went back to Kirsty Cameron, and the stubborn tilt of her chin. She's strong too, he thought unwillingly, and he realised that some of the anger he had felt towards her had gone.

That afternoon, when Laura was writing letters, Kirsty walked to the river, as Laura had suggested.

But I don't know that I would be calling it a river, she thought, sitting on a rock and letting her feet enjoy the coolness of the sparkling clear water. More like a big burn, really.

She said as much to Simon, when she met him beside the big white-washed building where the vineyard reached the house and its outbuildings.

Simon laughed, his blue eyes crinkling in the deep brown of his face.

'Well, now, Kirsty Cameron,' he said, smiling down at her, 'I'd like you to have a look at our river in the middle of winter, and tell me then if you think it's just a big burn. When it really rains, up there in the mountains, in the *kloof* that the house is named for, this "big burn" can sweep a bridge away, and it did, the winter before last.'

'What is a *kloof*?' Kirsty asked him.

'It's a narrow ravine—a sort of gorge—— Look, do you see that gap in the mountains there?'

'I could see it better without your arm so tight round

me,' Kirsty told him, removing the arm, which was resting round her shoulders, as he turned her head towards the blue mountains.

'I was just pointing it out to you,' Simon returned, unabashed. He looked down at her. 'Have you seen our cellars yet?'

'That sounds like a South African version of come and see my etchings,' Kirsty said.

Simon shook his head.

'If there's one thing I'm serious about, it's my wine-making,' he told her.

He opened the huge doors of the cellar, and took her inside, where it was dark, and cool, and slightly humid. There were rows and rows of wooden casks, and there was a smell that was, Kirsty thought, a little musty, but in a nice kind of way.

She said this to Simon as they walked along the row of wooden barrels.

'That's right,' he agreed. He smiled. 'Not just a professional way of putting it, but not bad. Red wine has to mature slowly, and it has to be in oak.' He touched one of the barrels. 'Not too easy to find coopers nowadays, to make the casks.'

'Coopers?' Kirsty said. 'When I was just a wee girl, my granny used to sing me a song about a cooper.'

She sang the few lines she could remember of 'There Was a Wee Cooper who Lived in Fife', and Simon, his momentary seriousness forgotten, threw back his head, laughing.

'Kirsty, you're like a breath of fresh air around here, just what Bloemenkloof needs,' he said.

Even in the dim light of the cellar, she could see enough of his face to know exactly what was in his mind as he moved closer to her.

'Sorry to interrupt,' Mark said coolly, from the door of the cellar.

'Not at all,' Simon said cheerfully. 'Kirsty, we'll continue the cellar tour another time.'

Quite unconcerned, he strolled to the far end of the cellar, whistling, his hands in his pockets.

I will not apologise, Kirsty told herself fiercely, for there is nothing to apologise for!

'Laura said I was to take a walk, there were things she had to do,' she said at last, telling herself it wasn't an apology, it was an explanation.

'Yes, she said so,' the doctor replied, his voice remote. He turned and walked towards the door, giving Kirsty no option but to follow him. He closed the big cellar door behind them carefully. 'I came back early,' he said abruptly. 'I was thinking about what you said, and I've sent the reports of all the tests through to Cape Town. If Bill Brown wants any more done, we will arrange that.' He looked down at her as they reached the wide steps of the *stoep*. 'I do want him to see her, in any case,' he said.

'Of course,' Kirsty agreed. And then, carefully, she said that she knew that Laura would be pleased not to have more tests done unless it was necessary.

Simon didn't join them for dinner that night, and the meal was, Kirsty thought, more silent because of that. There was a film Laura wanted to see on television, and when they had finished their meal Mark rearranged the set in her room so that she could sit up in bed and watch the film.

'There now, you've got your bell, so just ring when you want me,' Kirsty said. 'I promised my folks I'd write right away, so I'd better do that.'

When she had finished her letter, she looked in on Laura, but the film hadn't finished, and Laura seemed to be absorbed. Kirsty went back to her own room, and then out into the small courtyard.

The warm, fragrant darkness and the stars so clear in the sky were so different from anything she had known, she thought, standing close to the frangipani. To think that it was December, and Christmas only a couple of weeks away. It would be a very different Christmas this year.

Further along, a shadow moved, and came towards her.

'Kirsty?' Mark said. 'I was hoping you would come out; I—wanted to say something to you.'

It was the kind of voice, Kirsty thought, you would use to a waitress who had brought you the wrong order, or maybe to a char who hadn't done the cleaning properly.

'Yes?' she said, knowing she sounded as brusque as he did, and not caring.

'Don't take Simon seriously,' he said, standing beside her, but not looking at her.

'I beg your pardon?' Kirsty said, taken aback.

Now he looked at her.

'You know perfectly well what I said. He and Laura—it's always been understood——'

Kirsty didn't give him time to finish. Her rising anger erupted.

'By who?' she said—rudely, and ungrammatically, she knew as she said it. She took a deep breath. 'Laura certainly hasn't said anything about this—understanding,' she told him. 'But you needn't worry; I'm not in the habit of going overboard about someone being a wee bit friendly!'

'Now just a minute——' Mark began, but Kirsty turned away, unable to trust herself to say any more, and knowing, even then, that she had perhaps said too much already.

The big doctor's hand on her arm caught her, and swung her round.

In the warm darkness, he was very close to her. Kirsty could feel her heart thudding unevenly. He put his hand on her other arm, drawing her closer to him.

I should move, Kirsty thought, bewildered by the way she felt, so close to this man.

But she knew, even as she thought it, that what she really wanted to do was to move even closer to him, to feel his arms around her, his lips on hers. . .

CHAPTER FOUR

IN THE warm darkness a bell rang, shattering the silence, and shattering, too, the tension between Kirsty and Mark Barnard.

Without a word, she turned away from the man whose nearness had been so disturbing a moment ago. And this time he made no attempt to stop her.

But had he really tried to stop her? she wondered painfully a little later, when she had helped Laura to settle for the night, when she was in her own room, alone. Or had he done no more than put out his hand because he was so angry with her, because there was more that he wanted to say to her?

Perhaps she had just imagined the rest, imagined that his hand tightened on her arm, that he looked down at her in the warm summer darkness, that he was on the point of kissing her.

And that she wanted him to.

No, she hadn't imagined that. With painful honesty, she had to admit that that was what she had wanted, as she'd stood there in the dark, so close, so very close, to Mark.

And that is a very strange thing, she thought as she ran her bath, and got into it. Me not liking the man at all—in fact you could say close to disliking him, most of the time—and yet—feeling like that.

All at once it was disturbing, lying here in the bath, knowing that just along the corridor Mark would be in his room, perhaps doing much as she was now, having his bath, and—thinking about her.

And this was the most disturbing thought of all, somehow, so she let the water out, rubbed herself dry on the big fluffy pink towel, and put on her short rose-sprigged cotton nightie. Then, very vigorously, she brushed her hair over her head, and shook it back into place.

'Just you put the man right out of your head, Kirsty Cameron,' she told her reflection severely. 'This is just nonsense, to be thinking this way! And likely as not he won't even be giving you a thought, at least not the kind of thought that's in your mind!'

But of course, if you were being honest—and Kirsty did pride herself on being honest, most of all with herself—there was undoubtedly something about this man, she thought, with a measure of detachment, putting down the book she had been reading, and putting out her bedside light. He was not what you would call straightforward good-looking, with that very determined look to his jaw, but—yes, the high cheekbones, the lean brown of his face, the way he had of looking at you, his brows drawn together—there was something interesting, something that made you wonder what it would be like to be in his arms, to——

In the darkness, Kirsty could feel the warmth in her cheeks. All right, she told herself hastily, I'll admit all that, so perhaps the way I felt was just a—a natural reaction, you could say, a wee touch of chemistry that wasn't taking into account the fact that I don't much like him, and he certainly doesn't like me!

And, with luck, he wouldn't even know that she'd had such strange and disturbing feelings, thanks to the way Laura's bell had rung just in time.

Certainly there was nothing in Mark's manner the next morning to suggest that he had realised this. He was his usual cool and distant self, when they met as he was finishing breakfast, and Kirsty and Laura had just gone through.

'Remember, Laura,' he said, bending to kiss his sister's cheek, 'the physiotherapist is coming at eleven.' He looked at Kirsty. 'I'd like you to be with Laura, Kirsty,' he said formally.

'Of course,' Kirsty replied, just as formally. She would at some time, she knew, have to get some definite guidelines from him as to her hours of working, for, although Laura was obviously happy to have an easygoing arrangement, Kirsty herself would feel happier to know exactly what her official position was with this man. . .who was, she reminded herself fairly, her employer.

The phsyiotherapist was a brisk, forty-something lady with short brown hair and smiling blue eyes in a suntanned face. Kirsty liked her right away, and she was glad to see that Laura seemed to as well.

'I'm Meg Russell,' she said. 'I know your brother, of course, Laura; he refers quite a few folks to me.'

When she had shaken hands with Laura, she held out her hand to Kirsty.

'The nurse from Scotland—Dr Barnard didn't mention your name?'

'Kirsty Cameron,' Kirsty told her, and reminded herself that there was no reason why Mark should have mentioned her name.

Meg Russell's brown hands were gentle as she examined Laura's legs, turned her on her side, and felt her spine. Gentle, but competent and professional, Kirsty found herself thinking.

'Right, Laura,' she said. 'Now, what I want to do is to strengthen these muscles of yours, to keep them in good working order so that when they do take over they'll be able to cope. Kirsty, I'm going to show you some gentle massage that I want you to do on Laura's legs every day, and a little later I'd like to get you swimming, Laura. But before we reach that stage I want to use some of my machines on you. And don't look at me like that, my girl; they're all painless and in fact quite pleasant.'

She looked at Kirsty.

'I don't know how much physiotherapy you've come across, Kirsty,' she said, 'but what I'll be doing, at the moment, is fairly basic. Interferential treatment on the muscles, some laser on the spine, to start with, and gentle massage on these legs. Mark tells me you'll be

seeing Dr Brown, Laura; we'll see if he has any further
suggestions. Now, I'd like to have you through in my
rooms in Stellenbosch twice a week; how can we organise that? You drive, Kirsty? Good; I'm sure Mark will
organise a car that can take Laura's wheelchair—nice
one, I must say—looks as if it folds up easily.' She
took out a diary. 'Let's make the first appointment
early next week—say Tuesday, at eleven. That will
give Mark time to organise transport.'

Kirsty would have liked to walk to the car with Meg
Russell, to have the chance to talk to her about Laura,
but she didn't want to make this too obvious, and when
the phsyiotherapist said she would see herself out she
and Laura both said goodbye.

'She's nice,' Laura said, with obvious relief. 'Don't
you think so, Kirsty?'

'Yes, I like her,' Kirsty agreed. I like her matter-of-
fact way, she thought, even the way she talked about
the wheelchair, as if it was no big deal. With some
reluctance, she had to admit that Mark's choice of
physiotherapist was a good one.

Soon after Meg Russell had gone, Laura's friend Jan
arrived, in a bright yellow little Mini. Kirsty had met
her briefly in hospital in Edinburgh, before she and
Laura's other friend had been discharged, after the
accident. She remembered that red-haired Jan had
been bright and friendly, sympathetic to Laura lying
there in traction, with her leg in a cast, but talking
about the things they would do when Laura came out
of hospital, and came home to South Africa.

Jan was still bright and friendly, but Kirsty saw the
moment of shock in her dark eyes when she saw Laura
in her wheelchair. She saw too, and admired, the way
Jan pulled herself together and recovered.

But a little later, when there was a phone call for
Laura, Jan followed Kirsty out to the paved courtyard,
where Sarah had set out lunch.

'I knew about Laura being in a wheelchair,' Jan said
abruptly, awkwardly. 'I knew about it, so I haven't

any excuse, but—somehow it was different, seeing
her in it. I—I suppose I didn't really believe it until
then. Do you think Laura noticed that I was a bit
taken aback?'

'I don't know,' Kirsty said honestly. 'But don't
worry. What really matters is for you not to let it make
a difference—keep on coming to see her, keep her in
touch with other friends.'

'Oh, I'll do that,' Jan said. She hesitated, and then
went on baldly, 'But it does make a difference. We
all know that.'

Like Laura, this girl was only two years younger
than Kirsty herself, but, looking at the young, distressed face, Kirsty felt all at once much older than
those two years. Perhaps, she thought soberly, it's
being a nurse that makes you grow up a bit faster.

'I know, Jan,' she said quietly. 'And, most of all,
Laura knows. But try to be as normal as you can.'

And Jan succeeded in that, she thought, when they
were having lunch, by telling them an outrageous story
about a friend of her mother's who had been given a
surprise fiftieth birthday party with a male stripper.

'I don't believe you, Jan,' Laura said, laughing. 'I've
met Mrs Conran, and she'd be absolutely horrified,
she's so prim and proper.'

'I promise you,' Jan said, 'she enjoyed her party
more than anyone else did!'

'You're not telling me your mum enjoyed it,'
Laura said.

'I don't know about enjoyed,' Jan admitted, 'but
she's been talking about it ever since!'

Kirsty left the girls after lunch, Laura insisting that
she was to have some time off.

But this time, Kirsty thought, I'm not risking another
cellar tour from Simon. Not until I find out from Laura
herself just what the position is between them.

What was it Mark had said? 'It's always been
understood'.

Kirsty, changing into her bathing costume, and

picking up her sunscreen and sunglasses, sniffed.

It was just like Mark Barnard to have ideas like that. Someone should tell him that 'understandings' went out with the Victorians! People nowadays were into commitments, involvements, relationships, not 'understandings'.

But she was not, she told herself, going to waste this precious time off thinking about Mark Barnard and getting all steamed up. She was going to swim because she needed the exercise, with all this lovely food Sarah and the kitchen staff provided, and then she was going to lie and soak up this marvellous sunshine, and get some brown on her legs. First, though, some serious swimming was in order, so she had put on her old blue costume that went back to school days, rather than her bikini.

The pool was clear and sparkling, and it was incredible, she thought, this view of the mountains when you were swimming. It really was a bonny place. Not quite like any farm she had ever known, mind, with a house like that.

She climbed out of the pool, resolving to do twice as many lengths next time, and rubbed herself dry. There was a lounging chair, and she stretched out on it, her eyes closed behind her sunglasses, loving the feeling of the warm sunshine soaking into her bones, making her pleasantly drowsy.

She didn't hear anything, but a shadow falling over her sun-worshipping legs made her open her eyes.

A young woman stood there, looking down at her. A very elegant young woman, her auburn hair swept back from her face, falling in a deep wave on one side of her forehead. She wore a cream linen dress and jacket, and against it her skin was a deep and perfect golden. Through her big sunglasses, she looked down at Kirsty.

'I didn't know we had a guest,' she said, surprise in her voice.

Kirsty sat up, very conscious of her old and rather

shapeless bathing costume, of her pale arms and legs.

'We'? She wondered about that as she replied.

'I'm not a guest,' she explained. 'I'm Laura's nurse—Kirsty Cameron.'

The perfectly shaped eyebrows, raised, said more than any words could have done. There was only a moment of barely perceptible hesitation, and then the young woman smiled.

'I'm Helen Shaw,' she said, and she held out her hand. 'Mark's fiancée. Of course, Mark did mention that he was bringing a nurse for Laura.'

Mark's fiancée? No one had said—but there was no reason in the world why anyone should have, Kirsty told herself hastily as she put her hand into Helen Shaw's. And she wondered, as she did so, how this elegant young woman had managed to imply, without saying so, that of course she hadn't expected to find Laura's nurse sunbathing beside the pool!

'I wanted to let poor Laura settle in before I came to see her,' Helen said. She sat down on the chair beside Kirsty's, one slim golden leg crossed over the other.

'Poor Laura'? Kirsty had to force herself to keep quiet on that. Because pity was the last thing Laura needed right now. Needed or wanted.

She wrapped her towel around her, and stood up.

'I'm just going back now,' she said. 'Laura has a friend with her, but I'm sure she'll be pleased to see you.'

But she knew Laura well enough by now to realise that although the younger girl was polite, when Helen bent and kissed her cheek, she wasn't exactly over-joyed to see her brother's fiancée. And for some reason that she preferred not to dwell on, Kirsty found that that pleased her.

'Thank you for the flowers, Helen,' Laura said politely. She turned to Kirsty. 'You remember those beautiful roses I had in hospital in Edinburgh?'

Helen shrugged.

'I'm just sorry I couldn't do more,' she said. She sat down on the chair beside Laura's wheelchair, and took both Laura's unresisting hands in hers. 'I wanted to come with Mark, as soon as I heard how bad things were. We all thought everything would be fine when you got the cast off. You poor darling, how dreadful for you. But I couldn't leave things—this new manageress isn't quite up to it.'

'Helen has a boutique in Stellenbosch; she has some beautiful things,' Laura said to Kirsty. She rang the bell that was on the small table beside her. 'You'll have some tea, Helen? Jan, some tea before you go?'

Jan stood up.

'Thanks, Laura, but I'd better be on my way, I want to get back to Cape Town before the rush-hour traffic. I'll be back soon, though, and think about what we were talking about. Bye, folks.'

And that, Kirsty thought, amused, was because she didn't know what to say to the very elegant Miss Helen Shaw, didn't know what to call her.

A problem that was solved for Kirsty herself when Helen handed her a cup of tea.

'Now, do I call you Nurse, or Nurse Cameron, or what?' she asked pleasantly.

Kirsty felt her cheeks grow warm, but before she could reply Laura did.

'You call her Kirsty, of course,' she said, and there was an unexpected edge to her soft voice. 'Mark does.'

'Then of course so shall I,' Mark's fiancée replied smoothly. 'And of course you must call me Helen.' She turned to Laura. 'You are remembering that you're coming over tonight for a *braai*, Laura? I'm relying on Mark and Simon to do their stuff.'

Kirsty, watching Laura, saw the colour leave her face.

'I don't know,' she said, her voice low. 'I—I haven't been out much.'

'A *braai* is a barbecue, is it?' Kirsty asked, wanting to give Laura a chance to recover.

As she said it, she could see that Helen hadn't meant to include her in the invitation.

'Yes, it's a great South African tradition,' Helen replied. And then, politely, 'Of course you must come too,' adding to Laura, 'it's all friends, you know, Laura.'

'I know that,' Laura said after a moment. And of course, Kirsty thought, with compassion, that's the problem, having to face people she knows, and her in a wheelchair.

And that evening, when Kirsty went through to Laura's room, she found Mark there, trying to persuade Laura to come.

'I know I have to meet people, Mark, and I'm trying, but—but I'm not ready yet for a big *braai*, with all these folks, and people looking at me. I—I have to do it my way, and this is too much right now.' She saw Kirsty then, and the unspoken appeal in her blue eyes went right to Kirsty's heart.

'You don't have to if you don't want to, Laura,' she said gently, and she ignored Mark's dark frown. 'We can stay at home, you and I.'

'Oh, no, you must go, Kirsty,' Laura said. 'I want you to.'

'Not if you're not coming,' Kirsty replied.

'For heaven's sake,' Mark said impatiently, 'stay if you want to, Laura. And Kirsty, I think you should come; Helen did invite you.'

But not without my patient, Kirsty realised ruefully when she and Simon and Mark drove over to the next farm, where Helen's folks lived. But there was nothing she could do about that now, so she made up her mind to enjoy herself.

And enjoy herself she did, especially since Simon made it his business to take her around, to introduce her to people, to see that she had some of the delicious chops, a piece of the whole roast fillet, and some of the meat on a skewer, with dried fruit and onions.

'I love kebabs,' Kirsty said, accepting another.

'*Sosaties*, they are here,' Simon told her. 'Mildly curried, in the Cape Malay way.'

Once, laughing at something Simon had said, she was conscious of Mark's eyes on her, cool, remote. And when they were on the way home she said, a little defiantly, to Simon that she was grateful to him for looking after her.

'I would have been a bit lost, not knowing anyone,' she said, not caring whether Mark took this as criticism of himself.

'How did you enjoy it?' Simon asked.

'The food was lovely,' Kirsty said truthfully. 'But—but it would make a difference knowing people the way you two do.'

'We've both lived here all our lives,' Simon agreed. 'All the farming folk know each other.'

'I'll tell you something, though,' Kirsty said. 'All the men wearing shorts—I couldn't help thinking you all looked like overgrown Boy Scouts!'

There was a moment of astonished silence in the car, and then Simon burst out laughing. And so did Mark, his dark head thrown back.

And he looks and sounds almost human, Kirsty thought, taken aback by this unexpected breakthrough. Unexpected and unwanted, she reminded herself hastily, for it was nothing to her whether Mark Barnard laughed or not!

'Put the car away, Simon, would you?' Mark said as he drew up at the steps of the big old house. He slid out of the driving seat, and handed the keys to Simon. And his hand on Kirsty's arm was very firm as he led her up the steps.

And that, Kirsty thought, is just to make sure there are no long goodnights between Simon and me! She shook the doctor's hand off her arm.

'I'll just check on Laura,' she said coolly as they went inside.

'Yes, there's something I want to say to you about Laura,' Mark said. In the dim light of the *voorkamer*, he looked down at her, unsmiling. 'I thought you were all for encouraging her to be independent,' he said abruptly. 'If you hadn't interfered, she would have come tonight.'

It wasn't easy, but Kirsty managed to keep her voice steady.

'Independence is one thing,' she said quietly. 'Being forced into something like this—she isn't ready. Goodnight, Mark.'

She walked on ahead of him, and into Laura's room. But when she came out again, heading for her own room, satisfied that Sarah had made Laura comfortable for the night, she could see his tall form outlined against the window.

'Laura's asleep,' Kirsty said softly.

He didn't reply, and after a moment she went into her own room and closed the door.

Overgrown Boy Scouts, she had said. But there was nothing juvenile about Mark Barnard, she thought. And as she was falling asleep fleeting memories of the evening came back to her. Mark, with Simon beside him, expertly turning meat on the embers of the fire. Helen Shaw slipping her arm through Mark's and smiling up at him. Mark kissing Helen goodnight, when they left.

But it wasn't, Kirsty thought sleepily, what you would call a passionate kiss.

And then, unbidden and unwelcome, there was the memory of that moment when she had thought that he was going to kiss her, when she had wanted him to, with every fibre of her being. And that kiss—the kiss that hadn't happened—would have been passionate. She didn't know why she was so certain of that, but she was.

CHAPTER FIVE

'NO MORE tests, Laura,' Mark said the following evening. 'Bill Brown is satisfied with the tests that were done in Edinburgh. But he does want to see you.'

He had, he said, arranged to take her through to Cape Town the following morning.

'And Kirsty,' Laura said.

'Of course,' Mark replied, and Kirsty wondered if she had just imagined the slight hesitation. He's probably sorry he agreed to let me come to South Africa at all, she thought, what with me always disagreeing with him and arguing with him. But it's Laura I'm here for, and I'll not let anything else bother me!

They left right after breakfast, and Kirsty was amused to hear Mark and Laura saying how cool it was.

'We wouldn't be calling this cool in Edinburgh,' she said, 'and me in a sleeveless dress and sandals at nine in the morning. And no cardigan with me, either!'

'Well, it's the middle of winter in Edinburgh,' Mark pointed out.

'Even in the middle of summer, we'd be lucky to get a day like this,' Kirsty said fervently.

'It's going to be a strange Christmas for you,' Laura said.

And for you, Kirsty thought, with compassion. She saw the quick glance the big doctor gave his sister, and she knew that the same thought was in his head.

'Yes, it will be different, right enough,' she agreed. Last Christmas, she remembered, it had been raining. That sleety rain you got in Edinburgh in winter. Oh, yes, it would be different here in South Africa. Different and more than a wee bit strange, she thought.

'Look, Kirsty, the mountain,' Mark said.

Table Mountain rose into the clear blue of the sky,

rugged, the top smooth and flat.

'No tablecloth today,' Mark said with regret. 'But the south-easter is blowing, so you may see it by the time we go home.'

He's trying to be pleasant, Kirsty realised with some surprise. Pleasant and sociable. She didn't know the reason for the change, but she had to admit she liked it. Maybe he was feeling he'd been a wee bit hard on her. And maybe, she thought, I have been a wee bit hard on him too, a wee bit quick to judge him, with all the worries he's had about Laura.

The orthopaedic specialist had rooms in a private hospital just outside Cape Town. Mark parked the car, unfolded Laura's wheelchair, and lifted her into it.

'Are you going to be able to do this on your own, Kirsty,' he asked, doubt in his voice, 'when you take Laura for physiotherapy?'

'I'll manage fine,' Kirsty assured him. 'I'm pretty strong.' She looked at the girl in the wheelchair. 'And Laura's not very heavy.'

They were early, but the appointment before Laura's had been cancelled, the receptionist told them, and Dr Brown would see Laura right away.

Mark and Kirsty sat in the waiting-room. Kirsty asked Mark about the private hospital, and the doctors and specialists who had their rooms there.

'There are quite a number of these small private hospitals, or mediclinics, around the country,' he told her. 'I have a similar arrangement in Stellenbosch. It has a lot of advantages—there's a pathology lab next door to me, a radiologist on the same floor—I can refer my patients to almost anyone. This man—Bill Brown—is an orthopod, but he's discussed Laura's case with the neurologist upstairs. Oh, and by the way, you'll have gathered, I'm sure, that where specialists are Mr in Britain they're Dr here.'

Laura's case.

Kirsty knew, without anything needing to be said, that Mark's own words were echoing back to him.

Laura's case.

Because this was Mark's sister, his little sister, and Kirsty could see how close they were, the two of them, and them with no parents. All right, she herself certainly felt that Mark tried to control Laura's life too much, but there was no doubt that anything he did he did because he loved her.

The specialist's door opened, and a tall, fair-haired man looked out.

'Come in for a minute, Mark, would you?' he said.

Mark sprang to his feet. As he reached the door, he turned round.

'You'd better come as well, Kirsty,' he said.

A little taken aback, Kirsty followed him in. Mark introduced her, and the specialist nodded.

'Laura has been telling me how glad she is that you came with her, Nurse Cameron,' he said courteously. 'I was in Edinburgh for a couple of years, so I know what a sacrifice it must be to leave it. A beautiful city.'

'So is Cape Town, what I've seen of it,' Kirsty replied.

Laura seemed all right, she thought, although her hands were clasped together a wee bit tightly. But she smiled when she saw Kirsty looking at her, and lifted her chin.

'There's nothing that would justify interference in any way, Mark,' the specialist said. 'But you know that. I've just been telling Laura that right now the important thing is for her to have physiotherapy regularly, and to be patient. Let's see, it's mid-December now; I'd like to see you again in a month, Laura.'

Kirsty, pushing Laura's wheelchair, went back to the waiting-room. Behind her, the specialist was talking to Mark, his voice low. Kirsty could catch only a few words. 'No neurological damage. . .trauma of the accident. . .give it time. . .'

Kirsty looked down at Laura.

'Are you disappointed, Laura?' she asked gently. 'That Dr Brown doesn't have any answers?'

Laura looked away, but not before Kirsty had seen that she was close to tears.

'I shouldn't really have expected him to,' she said after a moment. 'And in a way I didn't, but yes, I suppose deep down I was thinking he would examine me, and say, This is the problem; an operation will put it right.' With difficulty, she smiled. 'You see, I'd even have welcomed an operation.'

Mark joined them. He must be disappointed too, Kirsty thought, for surely he must have had hopes about this man's opinion.

They had a cup of coffee in the small and pleasant tearoom before getting back into the car. But as Mark finished lifting Laura into the car he turned round.

'Look, Kirsty, the tablecloth on the mountain!' he said.

Snowy white clouds were swirling over the top of it laying a neat cloth over it. As they watched, tendrils of cloud billowed lower, down through the ravines on the face of the mountain.

'Quite a sight, isn't it?' Mark Barnard said.

'It is that,' Kirsty agreed. His hands were on her shoulders, turning her towards the mountain. She was very conscious of his closeness, and of the strange and disturbing effect it had on her.

Abruptly, his hands left her shoulders.

And that would not be, Kirsty told herself severely, because it bothered him at all, this closeness. It would only be because he realised he had got carried away, wanting to show me the mountain.

Laura was quiet on the way back, and so was Mark. And because of that Kirsty, sitting in the front beside Mark, had no option but to be quiet too. For half the journey. And that, she thought, was long enough for them to be sitting in the car saying nothing.

'You're in general practice, are you, Mark?' she asked.

'Yes, I am,' Mark replied, with a start. As if, Kirsty realised, his thoughts had been very far away. 'I did

think of specialising at one time—that's when I got
to know Bill Brown, because it was orthopaedics I
was interested in. But I realised in time, fortunately,
that it's the variety of being a GP that I enjoy. You
know—anything from ingrowing toenails to angina,
taking in babies, measles, even housemaid's knee!'

For a moment he glanced at her, and she thought,
surprised, how much younger he looked when he
smiled.

'Yes, I could imagine housemaid's knee would be
fascinating,' she agreed gravely.

'Of course, Helen thinks——'

He stopped.

'I believe you've met Helen—my fiancée?' he asked.

'Yes, I have,' Kirsty replied. And I wonder, she
thought, if she told him that not only was I lying beside
the pool, but I was in a shapeless old bathing costume
too? And her so elegant!

'Helen thinks,' Mark went on carefully, 'that I
should reconsider specialising; she thinks it would be
a much more civilised way of life than being on call
all the time.'

And that, Kirsty thought, was better ignored.
Instead she asked him how he had managed to organise
getting away this morning, and he told her that he
had an arrangement with another doctor in the same
private hospital to stand in for each other.

'But I'll just have to drop you girls and get off,' he
said. 'No, I won't stop for lunch, Laura—I asked Sarah
to have a sandwich ready for me to take with me.'

A strange girl, Kirsty Cameron, Mark thought as he
drove off.

Sometimes so prickly, so defensive. And so darned
interfering. Yet she had been really interested in his
work, and it had been very easy to talk to her.

And half an hour later, when he did in fact have a
patient with an ingrowing toenail, he had the sudden
surprising thought that he must remember to tell

Kirsty. Surprising and—disturbing, because there was no way, ever, that he would think of telling Helen something like that.

And that, he realised, was even more disturbing—to find himself thinking of Kirsty and Helen at the same time. And yet Kirsty had been amused, when he'd mentioned ingrowing toenails.

Ridiculous, he told himself, when the old man had hobbled out, with arrangements made to come to the clinic the next day, so that Mark could remove the toenail. Ridiculous, to think of telling her—she'd probably only been showing a polite interest, no more than that.

His next patient, Mrs Wingate, had been a friend of his mother's. Before his receptionist brought her in, Mark had another quick look at the letter from the cardiologist he had referred her to.

He stood up when his patient came in, seeing immediately the anxiety in her eyes as he asked her how she was feeling.

'Much the same, Mark,' she said. 'I'm still breathless, and I get tired easily, and, like I said, I think I actually felt better before you gave me these pills. I told the heart specialist that too.'

'Yes, beta-blocks can have that effect,' Mark agreed. 'Look, Mrs Wingate, Dr Durr found too that you have an abnormal ECG, and that, combined with your symptoms, and your family history—your father's heart disease—leads him to suggest that you have an angiogram.'

'An operation?' Mrs Wingate asked apprehensively.

Mark shook his head.

'No, it isn't an operation,' he assured her. He thought for a moment, wanting to make it clear to her in terms she could understand. 'It's a technique to show up any obstruction in the artery. Broadly speaking, Dr Durr will inject a dye into your veins, then he'll use a special camera to follow the dye, and he will see any obstruction.'

'And if something does show up?' Mrs Wingate said, still apprehensive. 'My cousin had to have a bypass done.'

'Yes, that's one possibility,' Mark replied. 'Another is a process of clearing the obstruction by——' He hesitated, not wanting to be too technical. 'By blowing up a sort of balloon inside the artery,' he said.

'Something like a drain cleaner?' his patient asked.

Mark couldn't help smiling.

'Something like that,' he agreed.

She wanted to know, then, if it would hurt. He could tell her honestly that it wouldn't hurt, although it might be a little uncomfortable, and she would have to be in hospital for a couple of days.

'Then I'd better have it done,' Mrs Wingate said.

Mark told her he would make arrangements with the cardiologist, and let her know.

'And try not to worry,' he told her. 'Whatever this shows, it's always better dealing with something definite.'

When she had gone, he rang the bell for his next patient, and his receptionist brought in a young woman, very pregnant.

'I thought our next meeting would be in the delivery-room,' Mark said.

'So did I,' his patient replied ruefully. 'But no such luck.'

A glance through the door as she came in had shown Mark that his waiting-room was full. A long and busy afternoon ahead, he thought with satisfaction. And once again he knew that this was the way he wanted his life to be. Unfortunately, Helen felt differently.

After Mark had gone, Kirsty and Laura sat on the *stoep*, in the shade, and had fruit and yoghurt for lunch, both of them assuring Sarah that that was exactly what they wanted.

'And a nice big pot of tea, Sarah,' Laura said.

A little later, she set her cup down, with decision,

and looked across the white wrought-iron table at
Kirsty.

'I've been doing some thinking, after Jan's visit,' she
said. Her blue eyes were steady. 'Jan's sister did the
course on remedial teaching that I want to do, and she
did it through Unisa—that's studying at home, doing
assignments, and then you have your exams. I'm going
to ask Jan to bring me Stella's books; I'll make a start
right away, and register for the start of the year. Will
you help me to get Mark to see that I really want to
do this?' she asked.

'I'll do what I can, but I'm not sure how much your
brother will want to listen to me,' Kirsty said honestly.

She refilled both their cups. Now seemed as good a
time as any, she thought, to ask Laura about Simon.

'Mark said you and Simon had what he called an
understanding, Laura,' she said.

Laura bit her lip.

'Mark would like that,' she said, her voice low. 'It
would be marvellous for Bloemenkloof, of course;
Simon is a very good farm manager, and he's built up
our wine reputation. I'm fond of him, and in many
ways it would——' She stopped, and then went on
carefully, 'It would have been ideal. But of course it's
different now—what kind of wife would I be for an
active man like Simon, and what kind of mistress for
a wine farm?'

Kirsty took both Laura's hands in hers.

'Surely none of that would stop you and Simon
marrying each other, if you love each other?' she
asked gently.

Laura shook her head.

'I don't love Simon, and he doesn't love me,' she
said with certainty in her soft voice—a soft voice that
suddenly had steel in it. 'And I will not have anyone
marrying me out of pity—not anyone!'

It was strange, Kirsty realised later, the way she had
said that. As if—as if it wasn't just Simon she was
thinking of.

As both girls expected, Mark was against the idea of Laura registering for her course in remedial teaching.

'Don't rush into this, Laura,' he said. 'Let's think about it. I do accept that you're keen to do it, but why not wait till January, and perhaps you'll be able to do your course at university, either in Stellenbosch or in Cape Town?'

Laura's cheeks were flushed.

'I want to do it this way,' she said stubbornly. 'Just in case.'

She looked at Kirsty, appealing, and now her voice was unsteady. 'Make him see, Kirsty.'

She manoeuvred her wheelchair out of the room then, leaving Mark and Kirsty facing each other.

Kirsty took a deep breath.

'She really does need to do this, Mark,' she said quietly. 'For one thing, it will give her something to work on—the days are long for her, you know. And——' She hesitated, wondering if she was wise to go on. 'And it is helping her to come to terms, just in case.'

'Just in case,' Mark Barnard said, his voice low and bitter. 'In case she is in a wheelchair for the rest of her life, you mean?'

Kirsty wouldn't let her eyes drop under the fierce anger in his.

'Yes, that is what I mean,' she said steadily.

For a long time his dark eyes held hers. And then, slowly, the anger left his face.

'I think you're very good for Laura,' he said, with some difficulty. 'And perhaps good for me too.'

Now what did he mean by that? Kirsty wondered, and her heart thudded unevenly, and she could feel warm colour in her cheeks, as he looked down at her. And what was it about him that made her so very conscious of him as a man, standing here close to her? One small step, from either of them, and they would be touching. Touching. . .

Abruptly, she turned away.

'Does that mean Laura has your approval?' she asked, knowing her voice sounded stiff and unnatural.

Mark shrugged.

'I suppose so,' he said. 'I'll tell her.'

Mark was out the following two evenings. With his fiancée, Kirsty supposed. On the second evening Laura and Kirsty were halfway through a game of Scrabble, when Sarah hurried in.

'We need the doctor, Laura,' she said breathlessly. 'I try to phone the hotel, but they say the people from the party Mark is at not there now, they go to someone's house.'

'What is it, Sarah, what's wrong?' Laura asked.

'It's Zita,' Sarah said, not quite steadily. 'It too early for the baby, but today she fall, and she don't tell me, and now the baby comes, and Mark not here to take her to the hospital, and Simon out too, and old Peter's car won't start, and Zita's bad, Laura; she's hurting bad.'

Kirsty stood up.

'I'll come and have a look at her, Sarah,' she said.

'And as soon as Mark comes I'll send him too,' Laura said.

'Is Zita your daughter, Sarah?' Kirsty asked as she followed the woman through the kitchen and out of the back door.

'She my brother's child,' Sarah said. 'But she's like my own—I brought her up, and I have no children. Just Mark and Laura and Zita.'

She opened the door of the small white-washed house. Another of the women who worked in the kitchen was leaning over a bed, and she stood aside.

The girl on the bed was very young, and her forehead was damp with sweat. Her eyes were closed, and she gasped with the pain of a severe contraction.

'It's all right, Zita,' Kirsty said. 'I'm a nurse, and I'll help you.'

She hoped that she sounded more confident than

she felt, for although she had been on a labour ward
for six months, that was two years ago. Swiftly, she
examined the distressed girl.

Sarah had said it was too early for the baby, but she
could see from Zita's size that she must be at least
eight months, so that made her feel better about having
to do a delivery here, if necessary.

And then, as another contraction gripped the girl
on the bed, Kirsty felt—— No, she thought, dismayed. Not breech. But there was no doubt about it;
it was a tiny foot she could feel.

Her dismay must have shown on her face.

'What is it, Nurse?' Sarah asked.

'Just that the baby's decided to come out feet first
instead of head first,' Kirsty said, determined to keep
her concern from the pregnant girl. 'That's all right;
I've delivered breech babies before!'

Once, she thought, and with Sister standing right
beside me, ready to take over if necessary.

'Now, Zita,' she said as Sarah wiped the girl's forehead with a damp cloth. 'You mustn't push until I tell
you. I'm going to help your baby out, and we have to
be specially careful because it's coming feet first. So
wait till I tell you.'

Gently, she probed until she felt the back of the
baby's knee, and prodded. The leg flexed instantly,
and so did the other, when she repeated this.

'Now, Zita,' Kirsty said urgently. 'Push. Push hard.'

She managed to grasp the baby by the legs, and
pulled firmly, until the shoulders were clear, but the
little arms were still inside, extended.

Zita was gasping with pain now. Kirsty tried to
remember everything Maggie Myles said, in the book
that was the midwives' bible. The essential thing was
to bring the head out slowly and steadily. She got one
hand under the baby, the other supporting its chin,
and suddenly it was clear, and safe.

'Cotton wool,' she said tersely, and someone—Sarah
or the other woman—handed her cotton wool. She

cleaned the baby's nostrils, and the mucus in the little
mouth, and then she blew into the tiny mouth very
gently. The baby cried, and Kirsty could have
cried too.

'Well done, Kirsty, you did a great job.'

She turned round, the baby in her arms, to see Mark
at the door.

'I just have to cut the cord,' she said.

The doctor put down the black bag he was holding.

'Sterile scissors right here,' he told her, and he took
out a small sterile pack. Kirsty cut the cord, and put
on the gauze dressing Mark handed her.

'It's a little girl,' Sarah said proudly. As if, Kirsty
thought, between laugher and tears now that the baby
was safely delivered, as if we hadn't noticed.

'Would you check her?' she said to Mark, and she
watched as he examined the newly born baby, his big
hands gentle on the tiny body.

'She's fine,' he said at last. 'Good strong heartbeat,
good reflexes. And a nice size too; we'll get her
weighed tomorrow. I'll take you to the clinic and both
you and your baby can see the doctor there, Zita,
but I think the best thing for you both now is to get
some rest.'

Kirsty, with Sarah's help, cleaned and freshened the
young mother, and left her with her baby in her arms,
promising that she would bring Laura to see the baby
the next day.

To her surprise, Mark was waiting for her outside
the little white house.

'I sent one of the other women up to the house to
help Laura to bed,' he said. 'I didn't know how long
you would be.'

'What is the time?' Kirsty asked.

'It's just after one,' Mark told her.

The night was warm and dark, and as they reached
the wide *stoep* Kirsty could smell the fragrant
frangipani.

Suddenly, as she put her foot on the first step, a

wave of exhaustion swept over her, and she had to reach out to steady herself on the stone balustrade.

'Kirsty?' Mark said sharply. 'What's wrong?'

'I'm just tired,' Kirsty said, knowing her voice was blurred. 'I'll be fine when I sit down.'

The next moment, she found herself sitting down on the big swing seat, with Mark beside her.

'Lean your head back,' he said firmly, 'and just close your eyes.'

You don't argue with a voice like that, Kirsty thought, and she did as she was told. She was never sure afterwards how long she sat like that, but slowly she began to feel better.

'I'm all right now,' she said, and she opened her eyes. 'I'll just go in and. . .' Her voice trailed off.

Mark was very close to her, in the warm darkness of the summer night. She knew that there was danger in this closeness, and she knew that she should move, should say something.

He murmured her name.

'Kirsty—oh, Kirsty.'

He was so close to her that she could feel his breath against her cheek. Then his arms were around her, drawing her even closer to him, and his lips found hers. Gentle at first, gentle and searching. And then not at all gentle, but demanding. Fierce and demanding and as passionate as she had known this kiss would be.

CHAPTER SIX

FOR an eternity, there was nothing else in the world but this man, his arms around her, his lips on hers. And her body responding to his, her arms keeping him close to her, her lips as searching as his.

Slowly, they drew apart. In the darkness of the warm summer night, Mark looked down at her.

'I think,' he said at last, unevenly, 'we had better go inside.'

For one moment, Kirsty thought he meant—— But Mark strode ahead of her, into his own room, and closed the door.

Kirsty closed her own door, and leaned against it. She could feel her heart thudding eratically, and her lips were still warm from his kiss. She put her hands up to her flushed cheeks.

And then, slowly, realisation came.

Mark Barnard had no right to kiss her, and she had no right to let him. He was engaged to Helen Shaw. He wasn't free to kiss her the way he had just kissed her. He wasn't free to kiss her at all, she thought painfully.

But how could I have let him? Kirsty thought. And then, with honesty, Not only let him, but encouraged him.

Her face felt even warmer now, with shame.

He'll think even worse of me now than he did before, she told herself. Not that he can think much worse of me than I do myself—and to think that I've always prided myself on not poaching!

And then, making her cheeks even warmer, there was the certainty that their kiss had turned the world upside-down for him too.

But tomorrow, in the sober light of day, how would

he feel? And how would he be towards her?

It would be better, she had decided by morning—and do I not look as if I didn't have much sleep? Kirsty thought, trying to disguise the dark shadows under her eyes—to get their meeting over as soon as possible. She left Laura still doing her hair, and hurried along to the small morning-room, hoping to find Mark there. Hoping, and dreading it too.

He was standing at the window, a cup of coffee in his hand.

'Good morning, Mark,' Kirsty said, not quite steadily.

He turned round.

He looks like a different man from the one who kissed me last night, Kirsty thought. His lean brown face was taut, and his dark eyes remote under the drawn-together brows.

'I wanted to see you,' he said abruptly. 'About last night—I'm sorry. It shouldn't have happened.'

She didn't know what she had thought he would say, or what she would say. Perhaps, she thought later, she had thought that he would say he couldn't help himself, but of course they must both forget that it had happened.

What she hadn't expected was a complete return to all his early hostility, all the remoteness.

Afterwards, she knew that what she should have done was simply to say that she was sorry too. And leave it at that. But she didn't do that. A foolish pride—she admitted that to herself later—made her lift her chin and look at him steadily. And smile.

'For goodness' sake,' she said lightly, 'it was only a kiss. No big deal.'

For a moment his eyes grew even darker.

'Yes,' he agreed levelly. 'It was only a kiss.'

Without another word, he walked out of the room. A few moments later, Kirsty heard his car start.

And really, she told herself sensibly, that was true. It was only a kiss. There had been plenty of kisses in her life before this, and, she was sure, in his.

But even as she told herself that a wave of desolation swept over her, and she knew that the truth was that she had never before felt the way she did in Mark Barnard's arms.

Later that morning, she took Laura to see Zita and her baby. They had already been for a check-up, Sarah told them before they left the house; Mark had taken them through to Stellenbosch early.

'And everything is fine,' Zita said, proudly showing Laura the sleeping baby. And then, looking at Kirsty, she said shyly, 'But Dr Barnard told them that it could have been very bad for me and for the baby if Nurse Cameron hadn't been here, and known what to do.'

'I'm just glad I was here, Zita,' Kirsty said. Gently, she touched the baby's soft cheek. 'She's lovely—what are you going to call her?'

'I already promised she would be Sarah, but I would like to give her your name for a second name,' Zita said. 'Wait till her daddy sees her; he's going to be so proud.'

As they made their way back to the house, Laura told Kirsty that Zita's husband was at university, training to be a minister.

'Sarah thinks the world of Zita,' she said. 'And she's been so excited about the baby. If anything had gone wrong, I don't know what she would have done.'

'Well, at least I've done something really useful here,' Kirsty said, without stopping to think.

'What do you mean?' Laura asked her.

Kirsty stopped pushing, and looked down at the girl in the wheelchair.

'Laura,' she said slowly, 'you don't really need a trained nurse—I do a little massage for your legs, I help you to wash, and dress, and I take you around, but I feel I'm here under false pretences. You—well, Mark is paying me generously, because I'm a trained nurse, but, as I say, someone less qualified could be doing this.'

Laura shook her head.

'You mustn't think that, Kirsty,' she said, not quite steadily. 'I need you—you do much more for me than these things you say. You—you help me to handle this. Please, Kirsty, don't feel like that. And don't think of leaving me.'

There were tears in Laura's blue eyes. Touched more than she would have wanted to be, Kirsty put her hand over Laura's, outstretched to her.

'All right,' she said. 'As long as you feel like that, I'll stay.'

One result of Kirsty's delivery of the baby, she found, was that she was no longer Nurse Cameron to Sarah; she had become Kirsty. And she was reprimanded, as Laura was, if Sarah felt she wasn't eating enough, or if she was too late going to bed.

It was rather a nice feeling, being accepted. And not only by Sarah. Somehow, Kirsty could sense a real warmth in the greetings from the farm workers as she and Laura walked in the vineyard. At least, she thought, with a bleakness that shook her, somebody out there likes me, even if Mark doesn't!

And, of course, there was Simon, always cheerful, always friendly, pleasant and easygoing.

'I'll take you through to Stellenbosch some night,' he suggested to Kirsty one day. 'Do you like Italian food? Good—there's a great Italian restaurant there.'

'I'd like that,' Kirsty said, meaning it. Now that she knew from Laura that there was no real 'understanding' between Simon and her, she felt that she could enjoy a casual date with him. It would be very pleasant to get around a bit, to get away from Bloemenkloof. Not that Mark was there very often in the evenings, at the moment.

'It's the build-up to Christmas,' Laura explained. 'Lots of parties, lots of folks entertaining—Helen has lived here all her life too, so she knows everyone. And with the boutique she feels she has to get around as much as possible. But they're having dinner here tonight.'

Kirsty was glad that Laura had told her. Not that it really mattered to her what Mark's glamorous fiancée thought of her, she told herself. But she had to admit that she was glad of the chance to give Helen Shaw a different impression from the girl with the old school bathing costume. There had been the *braai*, too, but on Laura's advice Kirsty had worn jeans and a T-shirt. Which, she had been glad to see, had been a good choice, as most of the women had been casually dressed.

Except that Helen Shaw's jeans had been designer jeans.

Not that it matters to me, Kirsty assured her reflection once again. And then, with honesty, Yes, it does.

Because there had been something—dismissive, condescending, somehow, in Helen Shaw's attitude towards her. She may be wearing Mark Barnard's ring, she may be elegant and sophisticated, but I can look good too, Kirsty decided. I can certainly look better than I did in my old shapeless bathing costume!

Something simple, she thought, simple but effective. She didn't have much choice, really, but there was the kingfisher-blue silk shirt she had bought in Jenner's sale, and the straight brown linen skirt Carol had passed on to her when she'd left the hospital to start a family.

Her hair was too short and too curly to be elegant, but it looked all right, she decided, and it was amazing what the green eyeshadow did for her hazel eyes. I don't have cheekbones like she does, Kirsty admitted to herself, but I'll do.

'Kirsty, you look marvellous,' Laura said when she went through, just before dinner. She smiled. 'Does Helen make you feel that your nose is shiny?' she asked. 'Is that why you've dressed up tonight?'

'Something like that,' Kirsty admitted. That was all.

Helen herself was wearing a cream silk shirt dress,

so simple that Kirsty knew it must have cost the earth.
Her russet hair was brushed back from her face,
smooth and shining. Her perfectly shaped eyebrows
rose just a fraction when she saw Kirsty. She said
nothing, but Kirsty couldn't help feeling satisfied.

'We're going on to the Colletts',' Helen told Laura.
'They always have a big do just before Christmas. It
goes on for ages, though, so Mark felt we had time to
come here first. I think you're looking better, Laura,
dear; you have more colour in your cheeks. I brought
you some magazines; they'll help to pass the time
for you.'

For a moment, Laura's blue eyes met Kirsty's. I
hope Helen didn't mean to be as insensitive as she
sounded, Kirsty thought, hurt for Laura.

But then, to her surprise, Laura winked, and Kirsty's
heart lifted.

'Thank you, Helen,' Laura said gravely. 'I've started
studying, but I'll enjoy having a break with magazines.'

Sarah came in with coffee, and just as she was setting
the tray down on the small table the phone rang.

'Probably for me,' Mark said, and he strode out into
the *voorkamer*.

'Remember, Mark, we should be going now,' Helen
called, but he was already out of the room.

'Dreadful man, your brother,' Helen said to Laura.
She smiled as she said it, but the smile didn't reach
her eyes, Kirsty thought. 'If he would just be sensible,
and become a specialist, he wouldn't have people
phoning him at all hours.'

Mark came back in, carrying his bag.

'Sorry, Helen, I'll join you at the Colletts' as soon
as I can—old Piet Marais has had a bad turn, so I'm
going there right away; I might have to get him to
hospital.'

'Oh, Mark, surely you can get Harry to go instead?'
Helen said. 'Anyway, the last time you rushed off to
see Piet, it turned out to be indigestion.'

'It might not be that this time,' Mark replied. 'He

does have angina, and I'm not prepared to take any chances. I know him, and Harry doesn't. Sorry, Helen. Just as well you came over in your own car.'

He kissed Helen quickly, and his hand touched Laura's cheek for a moment, before he hurried out.

'Coffee, Helen?' Laura asked.

'No, thank you,' Helen said, and her voice was cool. 'I might as well go on to the party; obviously I'll be lucky if Mark joins me at all.'

When she had gone, Laura and Kirsty looked at each other.

'She's not very pleased,' Kirsty said.

'No, she isn't,' Laura agreed. Her blue eyes were concerned. 'I suppose it's silly for me to worry—Mark's ten years older than me, he must know what he's doing, but—but I do worry. I just can't see Helen accepting Mark's going on being a GP, and—I don't like the thought of him doing something he doesn't really want to do, just because of Helen.'

Kirsty found it difficult to think of Mark Barnard doing anything he didn't really want to, but in fairness, she reminded herself, he hadn't wanted to bring her here with Laura, and he had agreed to that because it was what Laura wanted. So perhaps he would agree to something much more important, for Helen.

With Christmas only a week away, the old house began to hum with preparations, and delicious smells. Huge vases of hydrangeas, from the bank of bushes outside the house, appeared in the *voorkamer*.

'We call them Christmas flowers,' Laura told Kirsty, 'because that's when they bloom.'

Christmas flowers, what a lovely name, Kirsty thought as she stood looking at the laden bushes. And, bonny as they are in the house, I'd rather see them growing, like this.

She had left Laura working on some of the books her friend Jan had brought out to her, and she had decided, with regret, not to sunbathe today, for she had overdone it yesterday, and her shoulders felt too

tender to take any more. And it was too hot to walk to
the river, so she had decided to stay close to the house.

She could hear children's voices, from the crèche
run for the children of the farm workers. Laura had
taken her to see it one day, and she had loved the big
and sunny room, with bright posters on the walls, and
small tables and chairs for the children. All the pre-
school children of all the workers, Laura had told her.

Maybe I could look in there for a wee while, Kirsty
thought. The teacher had been very pleasant and welcoming.

The stable door had the top half pushed open. With
her hand on the latch, Kirsty stopped.

For Mark Barnard was there with the children. He
had his stethoscope on a small red-haired boy's chest,
and a little girl with black curly hair was holding out
a bandaged hand for him to see. He was sitting on
one of the small desks, and he was laughing. He had
taken his jacket and his tie off, rolled up his sleeves,
and unbuttoned the neck of his shirt. He hadn't
seen her.

'Come on, Thandi,' he said to the small girl.
'Andrew's fine; now let me see your arm.'

The little girl said something to him, and held out
a battered teddy, also with a bandage on his paw.

'Of course I should check Teddy first,' Mark agreed.
Solemnly, he took the bandage off Teddy's paw,
inspected it carefully, and replaced the bandage. Only
then did the child hold out her hand for him to see.

Mark looked up then, and saw Kirsty.

'I didn't mean to interrupt,' Kirsty said quickly. 'I
didn't know you were here; I just thought I'd come
and see the children.'

'Come in,' Mark said. 'They won't mind.' He turned
to the children. This lady is a nurse,' he said. 'Should
we ask her to help me?'

Most of the children, struck dumb with shyness,
nodded, but little Thandi managed a whispered, 'Yes.'

'I come in once a week,' Mark said, a little

awkwardly. 'It isn't really necessary, because the
District Health Clinic sends a sister round, but—well,
I've know the children all their lives, I know their
parents, and—I like to do it.'

'They obviously enjoy it too,' Kirsty said.

'Let's have a look at this knee,' Mark said to a
small boy with a large bandage on his knee. 'Almost
better—should we ask Nurse Kirsty to put a new
bandage on?'

The little boy shook his head.

'Not a bandage,' he said firmly. 'A plaster, Dr Mark.
A big, big plaster!'

Kirsty found a big plaster, and put it on, and the
small wounded warrior went off proudly to show his
friends.

'They all love plasters,' Mark told her. 'They'd have
them for hiccups if they could!'

Kirsty helped with the last of the children, now all
eager to have Nurse Kirsty see to them, and then
she and Mark walked back to the house together. By
common consent, Kirsty was sure, they talked about
the children, and the crèche, because that was easier,
and safer, than anything more personal.

The crèche, Mark told her, had been his mother's
dream, and she had started it a few years before
she died.

'Just in a small way,' he said, and Kirsty looked at
him curiously. With the children, he had been a different man, she thought. Younger—gentler—and he had
been laughing. 'But it's grown, and there's no doubt
that the kids benefit.'

He looked down at her as they reached the steps to
the house.

'Look in any time you want to,' he said.
'Aletta—Mrs Johnson—is always glad of people
taking an interest in the children.'

'I'd like that,' Kirsty said, meaning it.

From the huge cellar, Simon called, and Mark,
excusing himself, walked across to join him. The two

men went into the cellar, and Kirsty went up to the
stoep, slowly, and with a very strange thought gradually
surfacing.

Seeing Mark like that, with the children—it didn't
change what had happened between them, but it made
her see that there was another side to this man she
had told herself was hostile and arrogant. A side that
was very different, and very disturbing.

The estate car Mark had provided for Kirsty to use
was ideal for taking Laura's wheelchair, and he took
her out in it that evening, to let her get the feel of it,
he said, before she took Laura for physiotherapy.
Kirsty was pretty sure his real reason was to check on
her driving. Just as she was sure that his reason for
bringing Laura as well was less to see how Kirsty could
cope than to avoid the two of them being alone.

And that suits me just fine, Kirsty told herself.

It was a pleasant run through to the small town of
Stellenbosch, the next day, and Laura directed her
along wide streets shaded by huge old oak trees, and
past old thatched houses set in beautiful gardens.

Meg Russell, the physiotherapist, had rooms in the
same medi-clinic as Mark did, on the floor above,
Laura told Kirsty as they went up in the lift.

'Hello, Laura—Kirsty,' the physiotherapist said
briskly. 'I've booked you for half an hour, Laura; we
might need longer another time, but let's see how this
goes today.'

Kirsty had wondered what Laura's treatment would
be, and she was pleased when the older woman suggested that she come into the curtained cubicle to see.
First Meg lowered the treatment bed, so that she could
move Laura on to it easily.

'Electro-therapy,' she said as she fitted pads to
Laura's thighs. 'You'll feel a slight tingle—good; this
is just to give your muscles a bit of a kick, keep them
in working order. And then some laser treatment; it
helps bone and tissue healing.' She looked at Kirsty.

'You watch what I do today, Kirsty; next time you can do it.'

Kirsty watched carefully, glad that she would be able to take part in the physiotherapy treatment.

After that, Meg moved Laura's legs in gentle exercises, and showed Kirsty how to do the same.

'All for today,' she said. 'Next time I'm going to get you on your feet, holding those bars there. And I'd like to try some hydrotherapy. Your job, Kirsty, is the massage, and now the exercises.'

Kirsty would have loved to see more of the small town, to walk around it, but she could see that Laura just wanted to go home.

'Mark said to look in and tell him how the treatment went, but I—I don't want to interrupt him,' she said.

You mean you don't want to be taken there in that wheelchair, Kirsty thought with compassion.

Her unspoken thoughts must have shown on her face, for after a moment Laura smiled.

'All right, I'm not brave enough,' she said. 'Maybe next time.'

It was late afternoon by the time they got home, and the real heat of the day had gone. Rufus, the setter, came bounding to meet them, and after greeting them he ran into the house, barking loudly.

'He's gone to get his lead,' Laura said, laughing. 'He wants us to go for a walk.'

She looked at Kirsty.

'Take him for a walk if you want to, Kirsty—I want to phone Jan's sister to ask her something about the course.'

The thought of a walk was tempting, and when Rufus came back with his lead in his mouth Kirsty pushed the wheelchair up the ramp, settled Laura in her room, and told Sarah she was going out for an hour. Then, with the dog bounding beside her, she set off along the road that led towards the *kloof* that the house was named for. The *kloof* was the ravine, and *bloemen* meant flowers, Laura had told her. There were rare disas growing in the *kloof*, if you knew where to look, she had said, too.

But today it's just a walk I'm wanting, Kirsty told herself, glad to be able to stride out, for it was different walking with the wheelchair to push. The dog bounding ahead of her added to the pleasure of the walk, she thought as she reached the lower slopes of the *kloof*, and turned to look back down at the beautiful house, with its vineyards around it.

She had come further than she had meant to, she realised now as she whistled for Rufus. There he was, just ahead of her, heading for a copse of trees.

'Rufus, come here,' she called, hurrying after him. And then, dismayed, as she saw him, 'I'm so sorry. Rufus!'

For Rufus had found an artist, a young man with his easel set up. Or rather it had been set up. Now the bearded young man was rescuing the easel and fending Rufus off at the same time.

Kirsty hurried forward.

'It's all right,' the young man said, and she saw now that he was laughing. 'He was just glad to see me, weren't you, Rufus?'

He straightened up.

'You must be the nurse from Scotland,' he said, and now his laughter was gone. 'So it's true, then, that Laura is in a wheelchair, that she can't walk?'

'You know Laura?' Kirsty asked, taken aback.

It was a moment before he replied.

'Oh, yes,' he said quietly. Quietly, and bitterly, Kirsty realised. 'Yes, I know Laura.'

CHAPTER SEVEN

'I'M JONATHAN PAYNE,' the bearded young man said.
'I gather Laura hasn't mentioned me.'

It wasn't a question, but Kirsty felt she had to answer.

'No, she hasn't,' she said truthfully. And then, 'Did you think she might have?'

Jonathan Payne shrugged.

'Not really,' he said.

Kirsty hesitated, but only for a moment. This concerned Laura, and she had a strong feeling that it was important. And there was something about this young man—perhaps it was the beard, perhaps it was the long hair—that reminded her of her young brother, Gavin. Except that she had never seen dark shadows of—what? Loneliness? Unhappiness?—in Gavin's eyes.

'Want to tell me about it?' she asked gently.

'There isn't a great deal to tell,' the artist said. But he sat down under the tree where his easel was set up, and Kirsty sat down too. Rufus lay down close to them, his red-gold head resting on his paws.

'Simon said I could rent the old cottage,' Jonathan said. He pointed further up the rising slope of the *kloof*, and Kirsty saw the roof of a small cottage. 'It's a farm cottage, but they've built all these new ones, and they don't need this. I met Simon through friends. Laura and I met, and we—liked each other. We were friends,' he said almost aggressively. 'I mean really friends. At first. And then—well, we realised that we had become more than friends; we were in love with each other. And Big Brother didn't like that.'

Even under the beard, she could see that his jaw was set.

'He didn't feel it was right for Laura. You know—penniless artist, unable to keep her in the manner she's accustomed to, et cetera, et cetera.' He was silent for a while, and Kirsty waited for him to go on. He turned to her. 'Look, to be fair to Laura, she's a gentle girl, she's not used to standing up for herself, and he's always given the orders. He didn't exactly forbid her to see me, but he made it clear he didn't approve. I guess it all got too much for her to handle, so when her brother suggested she should go overseas, have a holiday, and think about things, she gave in.'

He looked away, but not before she had seen the bleakness in his grey eyes.

'We quarrelled about that, her giving in. And then she went away.'

He leaned forward.

'Tell me about her,' he said urgently. 'Is it true that she can't walk?'

Kirsty told him, quietly and factually, about the accident that had brought Laura into the hospital in Edinburgh, about the cast on her leg, the weeks in traction. And about the day the cast was taken off, and Laura found that she couldn't move her legs.

'But surely no one expected her to get up and walk, after all these weeks?' Jonathan said.

'No one did,' Kirsty replied. 'She would have had physiotherapy, she would probably have started with crutches, but there was no movement in her legs.'

Jonathan stared down at his clasped, paint-spattered hands.

'Spinal injuries?' he said.

Kirsty shook her head.

'No physical or neurological reason for the paralysis,' she told him. 'Only the trauma of the accident, and we all hope that time will help.'

She told him that Laura was now having physiotherapy, and she herself had been taught by the phsyiotherapist to give Laura daily massage, and gentle exercises. And she told him about Laura's decision

to start studying for the remedial teaching she
wanted to do.

'Good for Laura,' Jonathan said, not quite steadily.
'At least she's taking one step for herself.'

He stopped, and she could see how shaken he was
by his own inadvertent words. One step, and Laura
couldn't take even that.

He stood up.

'Will you tell her you met me?' he asked abruptly.
'Just say I—hope she's able to walk soon.'

Kirsty stood up too.

'Anything else?' she said.

He shook his head.

'Like I said, we quarrelled,' he reminded her. 'We
parted on pretty bad terms. So—just say that.'

Kirsty looked, for the first time, at the painting on
the easel. To her surprise, it was a view of the valley
below, with the old thatched house set snugly in its
vineyards. There was a slightly hazy, blurred look
about the painting that Kirsty liked very much. It
reminded her of Impressionist paintings, and she
said so.

Jonathan nodded, and said that he had been very
much influenced by the Impressionists. And then,
smiling, he said, 'You looked surprised. Is my
painting more conventional than you expected?'

Kirsty had to smile too as she admitted that perhaps
she had expected something more—— She hesitated.

'More way out?' Jonathan suggested. 'Actually, I'm
a lot less way out than Mark Barnard would think. I
have some pretty old-fashioned values. Like marriage,
for instance. But he didn't want to consider that as a
possibility for Laura and me.'

Kirsty walked briskly back down to the house, Rufus
running ahead of her. She had been longer than she
thought, because of meeting Jonathan, and Mark's car
was drawn up outside the steps. As she hurried in,
she could hear his voice on the telephone, from his
own room.

'You're out of breath, Kirsty,' Laura said, looking up from the notes she was making. Her wheelchair was drawn up beside the small desk—made of the same golden yellowwood that Kirsty had admired—and she looked businesslike.

If I'm going to tell her at all, it has to be right away, Kirsty thought.

She took a deep breath.

'Yes, I didn't mean to stay out so long, but I went over the river, and up into the *kloof*. And I met someone.'

All the colour had left Laura's face.

'Jonathan?' she asked hesitantly.

'He asked me to tell you that he hopes you'll be walking soon.'

Laura's blue eyes were on her face.

'Was that all?' she said.

'Kirsty—I'd like to talk to you.'

Kirsty swung round. Mark stood at the door, and there was no doubt, Kirsty realised, her heart sinking, that he had overheard.

'Mark, Kirsty was only——' Laura began.

'I'll deal with this, Laura,' he said.

He walked out of the room, and Kirsty had no choice but to follow him, through the hall and into his own room.

'You are interfering in something that is nothing to do with you,' he said flatly.

'I'm interfering?' Kirsty repeated, unable to stop herself. '*I'm* interfering? What do you think you were doing when you stopped Laura from seeing Jonathan?'

Mark turned away.

'I didn't stop her seeing him,' he said. 'I put my point of view to her, and I suggested that she needed time to think about it. But—I must admit I couldn't see Laura fitting in with his sort of life.'

'You might have given Laura the chance to decide that for herself,' Kirsty retorted, and she could feel her cheeks warm with anger.

'You don't understand,' Mark said dismissively.

'I think you're the one who doesn't understand,' Kirsty told him, and to her horror her voice was less than steady. 'So why didn't you do the whole lord of the manor bit, and send him away?'

She would have turned away with that, but his hand on her arm stopped her. As it had once before.

'Because Simon gave him a year's lease of the cottage and, hard as you may find to believe it, I do have some principles!' Mark flung back at her.

He looked down at her, his eyes dark with anger, his lean face taut. And in the middle of Kirsty's own anger there was a sudden and treacherous awareness of his body close to hers, of his breath, suddenly uneven, on her face. She knew, with complete certainty, that if he had taken her in his arms she would have been lost. And she knew, too, in that moment, that that was what she wanted him to do.

He shook his head, as if to clear it. And then, without another word, he walked across to the window, and stood looking out. For a moment, Kirsty stood there too, looking at the dark head, the set of the broad shoulders. Then she too turned away and left his room.

Before she reached Laura's room, she stopped, to give herself time to recover. What is it with this man? she thought, bewildered. Most of the time I disagree with him, I dislike him heartily. But the rest of the time. . .

She tried to be clinical and detached about it, to admit that there was a very strong—an extremely strong—physical attraction. But even as she thought that there was the disconcerting memory of seeing him with the farm children, laughing, relaxed. And the memory of the way she had felt, watching him.

'Kirsty?'

Laura's voice, calling from her room, was anxious.

Kirsty took a deep and steadying breath, and went to her.

'Was Mark very angry?' Laura asked.

Kirsty shrugged. 'I think it's got to be a bit of a habit, your brother being angry with me,' she said, trying to make her voice light and jaunty. 'Och, he's a wee bit annoyed, Laura, but I'm getting used to that.'

She sat down on the chair near Laura's wheelchair then, and, in defiance of Mark, told her about her meeting with Jonathan.

When she had finished, Laura was quiet, her face averted. And then, with one movement, she swung her chair away, across to the desk, so that her back was to Kirsty.

'I don't want pity from anyone, Kirsty,' she said levelly. And before Kirsty could ask her how she could be sure it was pity the young artist felt she began to talk about the plans for Christmas, and Kirsty had to accept that she didn't want to talk any more about Jonathan Payne.

Mark was glad he had house calls to make, glad to be forced to put out of his mind that strange and disturbing moment when, right in the middle of his anger, he had had to fight against Kirsty's nearness, against the memory of the way she had returned his kiss.

A kiss which should never have happened, as they both knew.

But—a kiss she had made light of, so it had all too obviously meant very little to her.

The small measles patient he was looking in to see was much better, and the chest congestion he had been worried about had almost cleared.

'I would say your problems are really beginning now, Mrs Benson,' he told young Teddy's mother. 'He's well enough not to have to stay in bed, but he's still infectious, so you're going to have to keep him entertained. I'd like to check his chest again in a couple of days, remembering that bronchitis he used to get when he was a baby.'

They left young Teddy bouncing energetically on his

bed, and his mother went to the door with Mark.

'And I don't suppose his sister will catch it till the
last minute,' Mrs Benson said ruefully. 'Just so that
they can stretch it out as long as possible. Anyway,
we won't have the same chest worry with her. Thanks,
Dr Barnard—see you in a couple of days.'

There were two flu patients after that, and then a
visit to Ken Harris, his multiple sclerosis patient. As
he had half expected, the remission hadn't lasted long,
and Ken's wife, Greta, had phoned, her voice carefully
steady, to ask him to look in.

Ken was in bed, and the slight blurring of his voice
when he greeted Mark prepared him for the other
symptoms now appearing.

'My legs don't seem to belong to me,' Ken said, and
he tried to smile. 'I have to lean on Greta to get
anywhere, and getting in and out of the shower is
tricky—can't manage the bath any more. I get these
dizzy spells, too, and I felt a bit sick this morning.'

Vertigo—nausea—loss of co-ordination—it was all
as Mark had expected, and yet the period of remission
could have gone on longer.

'I feel I should get up and get on with things, not
give in to this,' Ken said.

Mark had been checking his blood-pressure, knowing it would be low. He shook his head.

'No, Ken,' he said. 'Bed rest is what you need right
now. I'll be back in tomorrow.'

At the door, he looked down at Greta.

'I'd like him in at the clinic for a few days, Greta,'
he said. 'We'll give him ACTH, and he can have
daily phsyiotherapy, warm oil baths to ease the
muscle spasm.'

Greta's eyes were troubled.

'I can look after him at home, Mark,' she said. 'He
won't like the idea of hospital.'

'Look, Greta,' Mark said firmly, 'this will ease Ken's
problems, and it will give you a chance to rest a
bit—get a full night's sleep—so that you can handle

the next stage. I'll make the arrangements and give you a ring.'

On the way back to his rooms, thinking about Ken and his wife, about the problems that lay ahead as Ken's condition became worse, Mark had the sudden and disarming thought that he would like to talk to Kirsty about the way he would handle the future treatment.

And that young lady, he told himself severely, would no doubt have very strong ideas of her own, as she did about most things!

The next night, Kirsty went out with Simon.

No excuses, he told her breezily, he had already arranged for Sarah to stay with Laura, and Laura herself agreed it was time Kirsty had a night out.

Somehow, since she'd come to South Africa, Kirsty hadn't realised that she had been short on sheer fun. The place Simon took her to was run by an Italian family, he told her. The mother was at the cash desk, the sons and daughters, and cousins, were waiters and waitresses.

Perhaps, Kirsty thought, it was because she felt so relaxed, so easy with Simon that she could ask him how he felt about Laura as they drove back to the farm.

'I'm very fond of her,' Simon replied right away. He glanced down at her. 'If you're worried about Laura minding us being out together, forget it; she doesn't mind at all.'

Kirsty shook her head.

'No, I didn't mean that; it was just. . .' A little hesitantly, she told him that Mark had said there had always been an understanding between Laura and Simon.

'That was always more in Mark's mind than anyone else's,' Simon said. 'And of course now—— Look, if Laura and I were madly in love with each other, I'd marry her in a minute, but since we're not I don't think it would be a good idea,' he said honestly.

'Why not?' Kirsty said with determination.

He smiled.

'Because I don't think I'm the sort of guy who would do too well with a wife in a wheelchair,' he said disarmingly. 'Before this happened—— Like I said, I'm fond of Laura, and we could have had a pretty good marriage—we have the same background, we've pretty much grown up together—yes, it could have worked out all right.'

He patted her hand.

'But don't you worry about Laura and me,' he assured her. 'Laura certainly isn't crying her eyes out because you and I are out together tonight!'

And Kirsty knew that he was right.

'It was a super evening, Simon,' she said as they reached the big house just before midnight. 'And the food was magnificent.'

'We'll do it again,' Simon said. In the moonlight, he looked down at her as they stood at the foot of the steps. 'Goodnight, Kirsty,' he said softly.

His lips were warm on hers, and his kiss was extremely pleasant.

'Goodnight, Simon,' Kirsty said. 'And thank you—I really had fun.'

She waved to him from the top of the steps, and as she went into the house she was humming 'Come Back to Sorrento'.

Before she reached her room, she stopped as Mark came out of his room. He was in bathing shorts, and carrying a towel.

'I thought you would be later,' Mark said a little awkwardly. And then, 'You look happy.'

'I am,' Kirsty replied. 'We had great fun, Simon and I. We were at the Italian place—Pietro's.'

He looked down at her.

'I was just going for a swim,' he said.

'At this time?' Kirsty asked, surprised.

'I often do, when it's a hot night,' Mark replied. And then he asked, taking her, and perhaps himself, she thought, by surprise, 'Don't you want to swim too?'

'I think I'd like that,' Kirsty said after a moment.
A moment in which she suppressed any doubts she had
about the wisdom of this. 'I'll only be a minute, Mark.'

She hurried into her room and changed into her
bathing costume—choosing, without any conscious
thought, her bikini this time. When she reached the
swimming-pool, set in the middle of the furthest back
courtyard, she could just see Mark's dark head in
the water.

'There is an underwater light,' Mark said, 'but it
might shine in Laura's window and wake her, and
anyway, it's nicer swimming in the dark.'

The water felt smooth and silky, and warm, even
without the sun shining on it. Above them the stars
shone clear and bright in the deep blue canopy of the
sky, and the moon was almost full. Kirsty swam a few
lengths slowly, loving the silky feel of the water, and
the incredible sensation of swimming outside, on this
warm summer night.

Mark was swimming lengths, fast, but after a while
he surfaced beside her, his dark head sleek in the
moonlight.

'Best way of getting rid of any stress and tension,'
he said a little breathlessly.

Kirsty resisted the temptation to ask him about those
stresses and tensions. Instead she asked if he often
swam at night.

'Most nights, in summer,' he said. They were sitting
on the steps now, the water lapping gently around their
shoulders. In the moonlight, she saw him glance down
at her. 'Of course,' he said gravely, 'on my own I don't
bother with anything unnecessary like a costume.'

Kirsty was annoyed to find her cheeks growing
warm. But stronger than any embarrassment was the
unbelievable realisation that he was smiling. Almost,
she thought, teasing her.

She was glad the darkness hid the flush on her
cheeks.

'I'm sure that's a much better way to swim,' she
agreed, just as gravely. 'I've done a bit of skinny-
dipping myself, too, but only in rivers in the glen, and
even in summer the water was awful cold.'

They sat in a silence that was, she realised with
surprise, almost companionable, and then Mark
pointed out to her the Southern Cross, now low in the
summer sky. It was around then that Kirsty began to
think that perhaps it had been a wee bit foolish, this
midnight swimming, and the two of them alone
here now.

'I think I'd better go in,' she said quickly.

'You should swim again before you get out,' Mark
told her. 'Warms you up.'

She looked at him.

'I'm not cold,' she told him with complete truth.
And then, 'You do like telling people what to do, don't
you?' she said.

'Are you telling me I'm bossy?' he asked her, and
once again, unbelievably, there was laughter in his
voice. And this, she thought, bewildered, is the same
man who told me the other day I was interfering, and
I didn't understand about Laura.

'Are you not bossy, then?' she countered.

'Maybe I am,' he agreed. He looked down at her,
and now the laughter had gone. 'Kirsty, there's something I want to tell——' Then he stopped. 'Not now,'
he said, more to himself than to her. 'Race you to the
deep end and back.'

Kirsty never had been able to resist a challenge, and
besides, had she not swum for the school team?

They reached the deep end almost together, but as
they turned Mark drew ahead of her. It was when
Kirsty tried to catch up that it happened.

And why, she thought, dismayed, did I ever try to
swim fast in a bikini? For all at once she was swimming
topless, and with no idea where her bikini-top
had gone.

'Come on, you can still be second,' Mark said,

softly and breathlessly, from the steps.

Kirsty groped around unsuccessfully for a few moments. And then, slowly, she swam towards the step.

'You go on out; I'll come out in a minute,' she said.

Mark shook his head.

'You have to get out right after swimming fast,' he told her firmly, and held out a hand to her.

Kirsty thought quickly. After the talk about skinny-dipping, she was darned if she'd let him see that it bothered her at all.

Unconsciously, she lifted her chin. 'Just hand me my towel, would you?' she said very casually. 'I seem to have lost the top of my bikini.'

CHAPTER EIGHT

THERE was a moment's silence, and then, in the warm darkness of the summer night, she heard Mark begin to laugh.

'It isn't funny,' she said, with as much dignity as she could muster.

The laughter stopped.

'No, I don't suppose it is,' Mark agreed, but the laughter was still there in his voice.

'Beautiful clear moonlit night, isn't it?' he said conversationally.

He handed her her towel.

'Would you believe me if I told you my eyes were closed?' he said.

Kirsty wrapped her towel firmly around herself.

'No, I wouldn't,' she returned.

'You'd be right,' Mark said.

'What about my bikini-top?' Kirsty asked him, with a sudden picture of her bright, flowery bikini-top floating on the top of the pool in the clear morning light.

'Yes, now that's a thought,' Mark agreed. Then, relenting, he said that he would come for an early morning swim, and retrieve it.

They walked back to the house together, Kirsty uncomfortably conscious of the lack of her bikini-top. And conscious, too, in a bewildered way, of how different the big doctor had been tonight. Carefree—teasing—younger, somehow. And not at all hostile towards her.

As if answering her thoughts, Mark looked down at her.

'I don't know what it is about you, Kirsty Cameron,' he said. 'You argue with me, you interfere with things you shouldn't, you make me very angry. But you make

me think in a way I hadn't thought, and you make me
wonder about things I've done, and you make me——'

It was as close to an apology, an admission, Kirsty
thought, as this man was likely to make.

With his hand on the door, he looked down at her.

'Did Simon kiss you tonight?' he asked, taking her
by surprise.

'Yes, he did,' Kirsty replied.

The creepers growing over the pergola made it dark
here on the *stoep*, the moonlight unable to penetrate.
In that darkness, Kirsty was aware—very much
aware—of how close to her Mark was.

'You once said "it was only a kiss",' he said softly.
'Was that all it was with Simon?'

Foolish, and ridiculous, she thought, that she could
barely answer for the uneven thudding of her heart.

'Yes, it was—only a kiss,' she replied. And, even
more foolishly, she wanted to tell him that that had
not been true of his kiss. Only pride had made her
say that.

She felt his hand on her chin, tilting it upwards. His
lips were gentle on hers, gentle and warm.

'Mark—you shouldn't—Helen——' Kirsty said,
troubled, breaking free.

His lips were still very close to hers. 'There are things
Helen and I have to talk about,' he murmured. 'But
until then—didn't you give me to understand that a
kiss was no big deal? Changed your mind about that?'

He kissed her again, this time not at all gently. Kirsty
clutched her towel defensively. She wasn't sure, afterwards, just when she forgot about the towel, forgot
about everything but this strange and bewildering man,
this man who could make her forget everything but
being in his arms.

When they drew apart, he picked her towel up and
wrapped it around her.

'This time,' he said unevenly, 'I'm not going to say
I'm sorry.'

And I certainly could not say, It was only a kiss,

Kirsty thought, dazed, bemused, as she went into her room. What had he meant when he'd said that there were things he and Helen had to talk about? she wondered as she was falling asleep.

The next morning her bikini-top was on her window-sill, neatly folded.

Suddenly, it seemed to Kirsty, it was Christmas.

Everything was so different here—the preparations were different, the weather was different, she thought that was probably why the build-up to Christmas passed her by.

That, and, she had to admit with honesty, the fact that perhaps she had other things on her mind.

On Christmas Eve, she and Laura wrapped up presents for the children in the farm crèche.

'We're very conventional,' Laura said, handing Kirsty the scissors. 'Cars for the boys and dolls for the girls. But the children like it that way. Usually I go into Stellenbosch and buy the toys myself—I love choosing the dolls.' For a moment, her heart-shaped face was shadowed. 'This year I phoned them and told them what to send.'

She put the last parcel down.

'Good timing,' she said, and Kirsty's heart ached at the determined brightness in her voice. 'They should be about halfway through their party now; let's take the presents down.'

There were balloons, and jellies, and little cakes, and sweets, and about twenty small and very excited children. The presents were all labelled, and Laura called out the names, while Kirsty handed the children their parcels.

If it was possible, there was even more chaos as the presents were unwrapped.

'Look, Nurse Kirsty,' little Thandi said. 'Look at my doll; she's got pants on!'

The little boys were racing their cars, and the little girls were comparing their dolls, excitedly showing them to Kirsty and Laura, and then little red-haired Andrew ran to the door.

'Dr Mark, I got a Jaguar!' he said.

Kirsty looked up. Mark stood at the door, his jacket slung over one shoulder, his shirt-sleeves rolled up.

'Magnificent,' he said, admiring the car. 'I wish I had a Jaguar!'

Then he was down on the floor, being shown the other cars, helping to decide which was the fastest as the little boys raced them. And at the same time he was being shown all the dolls, and offered everything possible from small cakes with hundreds and thousands to sausages on sticks.

'I know we shouldn't go for the sexual stereotypes,' he said to Kirsty, when the party was over and they were walking back to the house, 'and we did try, one year, to give them something different, but now I think, What the heck? The little girls like dolls, and the little boys like cars, so why not let them have what they want?'

That evening Helen came for dinner, and for the handing out of presents to the staff, both the house and the farm staff, done before they had dinner.

'We always have the turkey on Christmas Eve,' Laura explained as Mark carved the huge turkey, 'then we have a cold buffet meal tomorrow—it's usually too warm to have a hot meal.'

Helen looked up.

'Mark says you'd rather not join us tomorrow, Laura,' she said.

Laura flushed.

'It's nice of your folks to invite us,' she said apologetically, 'but I'd just as soon be at home.'

Helen shrugged.

'As you please, of course. But I would have thought it was time you began socialising a little more. After all——'

'Helen.'

Mark's voice was very quiet, very even. For a

moment, Kirsty thought Helen was going to argue with him, then she shrugged again.

Across the big table, Kirsty looked at Mark's fiancée. Helen and Mark were going on to a party, and she was wearing black chiffon culottes and a filmy black top. The russet of her hair and the brown of her shoulders looked marvellous against the black. So did the heavy gold necklace she was wearing. She certainly knows how to dress, Kirsty thought unwillingly.

And why, she wondered, unwillingly? Why should she not accept that Mark's fiancée was a beautiful, elegant, well-dressed woman? Why should there be any reservations at all in the way she thought of Helen Shaw? But she could give herself no answer to that one.

Mark and Helen left right after dinner, and as they went out to Mark's car Kirsty heard Helen say, her voice light and amused, that at least they had got so far through the evening without a call for Mark.

Oh, dear, she thought, if there is one, Mark will be in trouble.

She and Laura had a quiet evening. They watched some TV—although Kirsty had to agree with Laura that it wasn't as good as British TV—and Laura wanted to go to bed early. Kirsty, having a last cup of tea out on the *stoep*, found herself wondering what her folks were doing, but realised, very quickly, that it wasn't a very good idea to be wondering that, with them so far away.

And I haven't ever, Kirsty also realised, spent a Christmas away from home. But what a foolish thought, she told herself severely, for a grown young woman to have!

But she had to admit, the next day, that it was a strange Christmas day. A hot, still day, the sky clear and cloudless from very early on, and soon the sun rising in the blue. And the mountains, with a blue haze on them.

And everything so quiet, she thought, for there was none of the usual sounds from the fields. Some voices,

some laughter, from the workers' cottages, but that
was all.

She and Laura had breakfast together, and they had
just finished when Mark appeared.

'Happy Christmas, Mark,' Laura said, holding out
her arms to her brother. And then, laughing, 'You're
bristly, Mark.'

'Sorry, I haven't shaved yet,' he said, rubbing his
hand along his jaw. 'Happy Christmas, Kirsty.'

'You can't just say it, you have to kiss her,' Laura
told him. 'It's all right, she won't bite.'

'I'm not so sure,' Mark murmured as his lips decor-
ously touched Kirsty's cheek. For a moment, as he
straightened, his eyes met hers, and she knew that
he too was thinking of that moonlight kiss, after
their swim.

Kirsty hadn't quite known what to do about
Christmas presents, but during Laura's last physiotherapy treatment she had managed a quick trip to the
shops in Stellenbosch, and got the new P.D. James
novel for Mark, and some L'Air du Temps perfume
for Laura.

'Lovely,' Laura murmured, sniffing her perfume.
'My favourite, and my other bottle is almost finished.'

'I'm going to enjoy this,' Mark said with satisfaction.
'She's one of my favourites.'

'Mine too,' Kirsty replied, relieved.

Laura looked at Mark.

'Will you bring in Kirsty's present?' she said.

Mark disappeared, and a moment or two later came
back carrying a small *kist* made of the warm glowing
yellowwood that Kirsty liked so much.

'A *kist*!' Kirsty said, delighted, kneeling down beside
it, and running her hands over the smooth wood. 'How
perfect. Thank you so much, Laura. And you, Mark.'

'It was my idea, but Mark had to get it,' Laura told
her. 'And don't worry about getting it back to
Scotland; we'll think of something!'

Mark left just before lunchtime, to join Helen's

family, and Laura and Kirsty had a pleasant cold lunch,
Kirsty assuring Sarah that she needn't stay, she could
go back to her family, and she would clear everything
back to the kitchen.

There had been a change in Laura, Kirsty thought,
in these few weeks. She had become more positive,
more prepared to assert herself, always eager for Kirsty
to do the massage and the exercises for her legs.

All right, she wasn't too keen on going to Christmas
parties and being among big groups of people in her
wheelchair, but that was understandable. She talked,
that afternoon, about the studying she would do next
year, about the exams she would have to do. And it
was good, Kirsty knew, that she was able to face the
possibility that her studying might have to be done at
home. Good that she had held out to do it at all, in
the face of Mark's opposition. But perhaps that was
one of the things he had meant, the other night, when
he'd said that she, Kirsty, made him think again about
things he had been sure about. Perhaps.

She had just made tea for them when Rufus barked,
and then they heard the front-door bell. Kirsty hurried
through the *voorkamer*, and opened the door.

Jonathan Payne stood there.

'I came to see Laura,' he said defiantly.

Rufus, overjoyed, had to be restrained from jumping
up to greet the young man he obviously regarded as
a friend.

Kirsty looked at Jonathan.

'I'll see what Laura says,' she said after a moment.
Her heart sank at the thought of Mark's displeasure,
but she couldn't just turn Jonathan away; she had to
give Laura the chance.

But Laura refused to see him.

'No,' she said, and she turned her head away. 'No,
I don't want to see him, Kirsty; tell him to go away.'

'Are you sure?' Kirsty asked.

'Oh, yes, I'm sure,' Laura said, a little unsteadily.
'Just—tell him to go away.'

Kirsty, relaying the message to Jonathan, could see that it wasn't unexpected.

'I suppose that's Big Brother's orders,' he said.

Kirsty shook her head, and told him that Mark wasn't there.

The young artist held out a parcel, wrapped in brown paper.

'Give this to Laura, please,' he said then. 'Tell her—— No, it doesn't matter.'

And in spite of the defiance, the hint of truculence, there was something a little forlorn about him as he walked down the wide steps of the big house. Kirsty, on an impulse, called to him.

'Jonathan.'

He turned round.

'Jonathan,' she said, wondering if this was wise, 'I think that when Laura said she doesn't want to see you she really meant she doesn't want you to see her. In a wheelchair. Does that help at all?'

He smiled, and she could see the man Laura had fallen in love with.

'Yes,' he said. 'Yes, that helps a great deal, Kirsty.'

Kirsty carried the parcel through to Laura. It was clearly a picture, and Laura, her fingers all at once awkward, unwrapped it. Both girls looked at it, the cottage among the trees, the sunlight dappling through the leaves and lighting the grass.

'It's the cottage,' Laura murmured. And, looking up at Kirsty, she told her, 'We said it would be our first home. We said we'd—— Oh, Kirsty.'

And she was crying, her fair head bent, her hands covering her face. Kirsty put her arms around her, holding her close, saying nothing, just letting Laura weep.

'I don't know why I didn't just have the courage and the strength to say I loved him, and I was going to marry him,' Laura said at last, her tears over. 'But—it wasn't easy, Kirsty. Mark was so sure I'd be making a mistake, so sure Jonathan and I were wrong for

each other. It seemed reasonable to do what Mark
suggested, to go away, think about things.'

There were still tear-stains on her cheeks, but her
eyes were clear now. Kirsty couldn't help feeling that
it was a good thing for Laura, bringing all this out into
the open.

'How do you feel about that now?' she asked.

'I didn't realise Jonathan would be so angry,' Laura
said after a while. She tried to smile. 'Between Mark
and him, going away seemed not such a bad idea. I—I
suppose I thought I could sort it all out when I came
home.' Now the young fair face was bleak. 'I didn't
know I would come back like this, though.' She held
out the picture to Kirsty. 'Put it in the drawer in my
desk, Kirsty, please.'

'You aren't going to keep it out?' Kirsty asked her.

Laura shook her head.

'It's over,' she said, and there was a determined set
to her soft chin. 'I will not have pity from anyone,
Kirsty.'

At the door, Kirsty turned.

'How can you be sure it's pity, until you see
Jonathan?' she asked. But Laura had turned away.

In the evening Mark came back, bringing Helen,
and Helen's brother and his girlfriend. Simon and a
few friends came as well.

Kirsty, knowing they were coming, had changed into
her pink dress. And never mind that it's short, and
the neck a wee bit low, she'd told herself as she'd
brushed her hair and put on some perfume. It looks
good, especially now that I'm quite brown.

She'd helped Laura to change into silky pleated
trousers and a sleeveless top just the blue of her eyes.
Laura's fair hair was long enough now to be piled on
top of her head.

'How do you feel about tonight, Laura?' Kirsty had
asked, her eyes meeting Laura's in the mirror.

'I'm not mad about the idea,' Laura had admitted.
Then, determinedly, she'd smiled. 'But it's all folks I

know, and it's in my own home. But I'm glad you're here, Kirsty.'

Well, Kirsty had told herself, maybe it's not what I would be calling real nursing, but there's no doubt that right now Laura does need me.

There was a buffet supper, and after that Simon took charge of the music, and someone rolled back the carpet in the *voorkamer*—what a way to treat what was surely a real Persian carpet, Kirsty thought—and there was talk and laughter. Kirsty danced a lot—Laura insisting that she was to take the chance—but every so often she went back to sit with Laura, saying quite truthfully that she needed to catch her breath.

It must have been around midnight, and she was on her way to join Laura, when she saw that one of Simon's friends was sitting talking to her. All the doors were open, and Kirsty went out on to the *stoep*.

It was a perfect evening, the moon high in the cloudless sky, the stars clear and bright. And it was warm, still, with a gentler warmth than the heat of the day.

Beautiful, Kirsty told herself. Magic.

And suddenly, without any warning, she would have given up all of this beauty to be in Edinburgh on a cold and rainy night, and knowing she was only an hour away from her folks.

There was a movement beside her.

'Tears, Kirsty?' Mark said gently.

He took out his handkerchief and dried the tears on her cheeks, his big hands awkward.

'Are you homesick?' he asked, and the warm concern in his voice unnerved her completely.

'Just a wee bit,' she said. 'I—I just got to thinking how far away my folks are, and—och, it was silly, really.'

'Not at all silly,' Mark assured her. He looked down at her. 'You're lucky, Kirsty, to have your family to be close to. Wouldn't you like to phone them, just to say Happy Christmas?'

Kirsty shook her head.

'Oh, no,' she said, with certainty. 'I would just cry, and my mum would cry, and that would be an awful waste of money!'

Mark burst out laughing, his dark head thrown back.

'Well, it's nice to know Scots folk really are careful with money,' he said at last. He took her hand. 'Are you ready to come back in?' he asked her.

'Do I look as if I've been crying?' Kirsty asked him anxiously.

In the moonlight, he looked down at her.

'You look fine to me,' he said, and there was something strange in his voice, something that made Kirsty think it would probably be a very good idea for the two of them to go inside right now, to join the others, in the big, noisy party.

'Mark——' she began, not quite steadily, but before she could say any more there was the sound of running feet, and one of the farm workers passed them without seeing them as he rang the big bell at the front door.

Mark hurried towards him, Kirsty behind him.

'Henry? Is something wrong?'

The man turned to him.

'Dr Mark, I was coming for you—it's old Peter—he's bad, real bad; he's bleeding so much, and no one knew until Sarah went to take him some food. Come quick, Dr Mark!'

'I'll get my bag,' Mark said. And to Kirsty, briefly, 'Peter has an ulcer; this sounds bad.'

He disappeared into the house, and a moment or two later he was back, his bag in his hand.

And Helen behind him.

'For heaven's sake, Mark,' she said impatiently. 'Send for an ambulance; he'll probably have to be taken to hospital anyway.'

'An ambulance could take too long,' Mark said, without looking at her. 'Right, Henry, let's go.'

Kirsty stepped forward.

'Can I help, Mark?' she asked him.

At the foot of the steps, he turned round.

'Yes,' he said right away. 'Yes, I might have to set up a drip. I'd be glad of your help, Kirsty.'

Kirsty hurried after the two men, all too conscious, as she caught up with them, of Helen Shaw standing at the open door watching them.

CHAPTER NINE

THERE was no time to waste, Mark could see that immediately. The old man was barely conscious. He had lost a great deal of blood, and he was obviously in severe pain.

'Go back to the house and tell Simon to phone for the ambulance,' Mark told the man who had come up for him. He touched the old man's shoulder gently. 'You'll have to go to hospital, Peter, but Nurse Cameron and I will make you more comfortable now.'

Old Peter's eyes flickered, and he managed to nod. And as Mark prepared an injection he had a sudden memory of long ago, when he was a child, and this old man was so much younger, and he had helped Mark to make a cart with wheels, his brown hands sure and steady. And now—— Mark looked at his own hands, knowing that he had to keep emotion and sentiment back, knowing that now his own hands needed that same sureness.

'Pethidine, just enough to ease the pain,' he said to Kirsty, his voice low. 'Now we'll give him some Maintelyte, to restore the electrolyte balance.'

It was strange how well they worked together, he thought fleetingly as they set up the drip and worked to stabilise the old man. Kirsty seemed to know instinctively what he wanted her to do, where her own hands were needed. Old Peter had lost so much blood, though, that his pulse was still thready and his blood-pressure dangerously low even after the drip was operating.

Silently, they worked together, and, although this was the first time, Mark knew that they were a team, he and Kirsty.

'It isn't going any lower; we're holding him,' he said

an hour later, and he could hear the weariness in his
own voice, could see it mirrored in Kirsty's face. 'I
hope the ambulance comes soon; he desperately needs
a blood transfusion, and surgical intervention.'

'If he doesn't get that soon—chemical peritonitis,
and bacterial peritonitis,' Kirsty murmured.

She looked at him.

'If you hadn't been able to set up the drip,
and prevent him going completely into shock, he
wouldn't have stood much of a chance,' she said, her
voice low.

'Over the years I've learned that all sorts of medical
emergencies can happen on the farm,' Mark said, his
eyes on the old man on the bed. 'And the ambulances
will be busy tonight; I couldn't risk waiting.'

He looked up, and for a moment Kirsty's hazel eyes
met his. And Mark knew that she was remembering
Helen's impatience, and how she had urged him just
to send for the ambulance. Which would almost certainly have been too late for old Peter. Not, of course,
that there had been any question of him doing as Helen
wanted. For a moment, a little foolishly, he was glad
that Kirsty had seen that.

'Ambulance here now, Dr Mark,' Henry said,
coming into the room.

A moment later the ambulance men came in, and
Mark supervised as they eased the old man on to the
stretcher.

'What do you think, Mark?' Kirsty asked as they
walked back to the house together, the lights of the
ambulance disappearing round the corner of the drive
ahead of them.

'He should make it,' Mark said after a moment. 'I
think we got him in time, and they'll operate right
away.' He hesitated, but only for a moment. 'I've
known old Peter all my life. He's Sarah's cousin—he
helped me to make a cart, and he taught me to ride
a bike.'

In the warm summer darkness, Kirsty's small hand

came out and touched his. Without any need for
thought, Mark's own hand closed on hers.

'Thanks, Kirsty,' he said. 'For the sympathy, but
also for doing a good job. It made all the difference,
having you there.'

All the cars had gone, and the house was silent, only
a dim light shining in the small morning-room. The
party was over, and the guests had gone. Including
Helen. And she must have been very angry, Mark
thought, at yet another evening spoiled—in her
opinion. No doubt she would have another try at per-
suading him that life as a specialist would be better
than life as a GP.

There was a tray with sandwiches and a flask of
coffee waiting for them, and a note from Sarah to say
she had put Laura to bed.

Kirsty poured two mugs of coffee, and it was only
when she handed him one that Mark saw the dark
shadows of weariness under her eyes. They ate a sandwich each and drank some coffee in silence. But it
wasn't an uncomfortable silence, Mark found himself
thinking. Rather a closeness between two people who
had worked well together.

He leaned back and closed his eyes. After a moment,
Kirsty touched his arm.

'Go to bed, Mark,' she said softly. 'You're
exhausted.'

He opened his eyes and looked at her.

'So are you,' he returned. 'We're both tired.'

He stood up, and so did she. Somehow, when she
was close to him, he was taken aback to find once
again what a little thing she was.

'Goodnight, Kirsty,' he said, outside his door. 'I'm
glad you were here to help me.'

I mean that, he thought as he went into his room.
For it was perhaps the first time the two of them had
had no undercurrents, no complications at all, in their
relationship.

It would be good, he thought drowsily as he

was falling asleep, if it could always be like that
between them.

Kirsty slept like the proverbial log, but the moment
she woke she wondered how old Peter was. Mark
phoned the hospital before he had breakfast, and came
back to tell Kirsty and Laura that Peter had come
through the operation reasonably well.

'He's not a young man, of course, and he had lost
a great deal of blood, but unless anything goes wrong
he should make it,' he said.

Later, Laura told Kirsty that Helen had been
very angry, and had barely spoken to her before
she left.

'Other than to tell me to remind Mark about the
party they're going to tonight,' she said.

'Poor man,' Kirsty said involuntarily. 'Another
party, and him up half the night last night, and away
to see some of his patients today.'

Laura looked at her, and there was a question in
her blue eyes that brought a wave of colour to Kirsty's
cheeks and made her change the subject hastily.

The next day she took Laura to Stellenbosch for her
twice-weekly physiotherapy session. Meg Russell had
obviously won Laura's confidence, and today the
physiotherapist was to try something new.

At the far end of the treatment-rooms there was
some exercise equipment. Meg pushed Laura's wheelchair between two parallel bars.

'Now,' she said briskly, 'hold on at each side and
lift yourself up, Laura. Come on, there's nothing wrong
with your arms; they're strong enough.'

Slowly, her face intent, Laura managed to raise herself. Then Meg Russell moved the wheelchair away,
so that Laura's legs were touching the ground.

'I don't want you to do anything, Laura,' the phsyiotherapist said reassuringly. 'Just stay there for a little
while. Let your legs get used to being in the position
they should be.' She and Kirsty were close to Laura,

but Laura managed to hold on, to keep herself upright.

'Good girl. That's enough for today; we'll have some laser and then some interferential now,' Meg said briskly, and she pushed the wheelchair back and helped Laura to sit in it. 'Right, Kirsty, you can do the laser on your own today; you did a nice job under my supervision last time.'

Kirsty held the small instrument carefully, and moved it gently on Laura's spine, as Meg had shown her.

'It's a bit like doing ironing,' she said, 'except that this is cold ironing.'

'I hadn't thought of it like that,' the phsyiotherapist said, and she smiled. 'Right, you go on ironing until the bell rings.'

Kirsty, waiting while Laura had the rest of her treatment, looked at the row of books above the desk. Most of them were phsyiotherapy manuals, but to her surprise she saw a heavy medical textbook she recognised, and a Maggie Myles. The phsyiotherapist, coming out of Laura's cubicle then, saw her looking at them.

'Yes, I qualified as a nurse before I trained in physiotherapy,' she said 'And I still sometimes find my old nursing books useful for looking something up.'

'Some parts of that one I knew off by heart,' Kirsty said, looking at the heavy textbook of medical-surgical nursing. 'And of course Maggie Myles is still every midwife's bible.'

Meg Russell agreed with that, and then she went on to say that she thought Laura should have some hydrotherapy, and she would come out to Bloemenkloof the next day, to show Kirsty what should be done.

'I was talking about it to Mark, and he says you're a good swimmer,' the physiotherapist said. Kirsty, thinking of the only time Mark had had anything to do with her swimming, felt her cheeks grow warm. 'We'll see how it goes but it could be worthwhile getting Laura into the pool every day, even for a short time.'

When Laura's session was over, and they were waiting for the lift to take them to the parking garage, Laura looked up at Kirsty.

'Let's go out into the street before we go back,' she said. 'It—it's about time I had a more public outing than just around the farm.'

'Fine,' Kirsty replied, keeping her voice casual. 'That's a good idea. Just tell me when you've had enough.'

They walked down Dorp Street, and Kirsty exclaimed at the wide, oak-shaded street with its water-furrows, and its old buildings, many of them thatched. Once, a woman on the other side of the street recognised Laura.

'Nice to see you out, Laura.'

For a moment it looked as if she would cross to them, but Kirsty, seeing the sudden panic on Laura's face, pushed the wheelchair on quickly, so that Laura was able to wave and say hello, and no more.

'I think we'll go back now, Kirsty,' Laura said, a little further on down the street. 'Next time we'll let you see the Brak—it's a sort of town square, with a little arsenal, and a couple of churches, if you're into old things you——'

Her voice broke off.

Kirsty, busy turning the wheelchair back the way they had come, saw immediately why.

Jonathan Payne was coming towards them, some paintings under his arm. There was no way of avoiding him, and anyway, she could see by the determination on his face that he was not about to let himself be avoided.

'Hello, Laura,' he said quietly, looking down at the girl in the wheelchair. 'Hello, Kirsty. I was just taking some paintings to the Libertas Gallery; they've sold a few for me.'

'Hello, Jonathan,' Laura said. And then she asked,

her chin lifted, 'Aren't you heading the wrong way for the gallery?'

Unexpectedly, Jonathan smiled.

'Yes, I am,' he agreed. 'But I saw you in the distance.'

'And recognised me by the wheelchair,' Laura said flatly, adding before Jonathan could reply to that, 'Thank you for the painting; it's beautiful.'

'I wanted you to have it,' Jonathan said to her. 'Laura——'

Laura broke in.

'I'm afraid we have to go; we're late,' she said quickly. The young artist put his hand on hers, which were clasped together tightly.

'Can I see you again, Laura? Soon?'

Laura pulled her hands away from him and turned away.

'I don't know,' she said shakily. 'I don't think it's a good idea Jonathan.'

'Why not?' he said, but Laura only shook her head.

'We're going,' Kirsty said, coming into the conversation for the first time. Because enough is enough, she thought, looking at Laura's face, white and distressed.

She pushed the wheelchair briskly back to the clinic, and only when they were in the car and headed for home did she feel that something should be said about the meeting.

'That was unfortunate, Laura,' she said carefully. 'It obviously upset you—I'm sorry about that.'

'I had to see him sooner or later, I suppose,' Laura said. She was still, Kirsty saw with a quick glance, looking very distressed. 'I suppose I'm a coward, Kirsty, not wanting people to see me, and, most of all, not wanting Jonathan to see me. I just don't think I could face trouble with Mark about Jonathan.' She tried to smile. 'Or trouble with Jonathan about Mark. It's all too much for me.' The fleeting smile was gone. 'And anyway, I don't want pity from anyone.'

'It's all too much for me'.

Perhaps, Kirsty thought later, it was then that she began to wonder. At first her thoughts were vague, and only gradually did they begin to take form.

'It's all too much for me', Laura had said now. And Jonathan, the day she met him, what had he said? 'I guess it all got too much for her to handle'. And Laura had said, too, that going away hadn't seemed a bad idea. Going away, Kirsty thought, from all her problems. Then there had been the accident, and all those weeks when her leg was in a cast, and in traction. But they had been weeks when she didn't have to face any of the problems she had been glad to leave behind. Problems that would, of course, return when she was out of hospital, and on her feet again, and able to go home.

Late that night, Kirsty sat at her open window, thinking about this, and gradually the answer came to her. At least, she was almost certain it was the answer.

It wouldn't, of course, be any conscious thought; it would be a buried realisation that all the old problems would be there when she was on her feet again. Of course, if she wasn't on her feet, she wouldn't have to do anything about any of these problems.

Hysterical paralysis. Could that be it?

If only I had a good textbook, Kirsty thought. There would be a section on psychosomatic problems, and she was sure there would be something about hysterical paralysis.

If Mark had been at home, she would have gone to him right away, to tell him what she had been thinking. But he was out, and by morning Kirsty had come to see that she should think about this before she spoke to him. Think about it, and try to find out something more.

Because, she thought ruefully, Mum and Gran have always said I have a tendency to speak first and think second.

Meg Russell, the physiotherapist, had a textbook;

she would look at that the next time she took
Laura there.

The weather had been growing hotter each day, and
the fields of ripening grapes had to be irrigated regularly. Kirsty, returning Simon's wave as they passed
one of the fields that morning, said to Laura that he
didn't seem his usual cheerful self.

'He's worried about the weather,' Laura told her.
She looked up at the deep blue of the sky. 'If we
get a summer storm—and we could, with this sort of
build-up—there's a real risk of losing the whole crop,
at this stage.'

'And here I am every morning just thinking it's
another lovely day,' Kirsty said, sobered by this.

'Well, it may not happen. If the south-easter blows
in Cape Town, we're not likely to get rain,' Laura said.
'I must say, since it's as hot as this, I'm looking forward
to getting into the pool this afternoon when
Meg comes.'

And that wasn't entirely true, Kirsty knew. By now
she knew Laura well enough to be able to recognise
the signs of strain on her face, the voice that was a
little too bright, the smile that needed some effort.
And of course, she reminded herself, just trying to do
something new would be another reminder to Laura
of her condition.

'We're going to start gently, Laura,' the phsyiotherapist said that afternoon, when the three of them were
in the pool. 'See, even getting you in wasn't too difficult—Kirsty, you'll manage, won't you? While you're
sitting on the steps, the water is holding your legs up.
Now I'm going to move you one step down, and you're
going to lift yourself up on your hands. Good, that's it.'

After that, Meg got Laura to use a small board, and
to swim using that. For a moment Kirsty, watching,
thought she saw movement in Laura's legs, but it was
only the ripple of the water.

'Every day, if possible,' the phsyiotherapist said
briskly when she left. 'Best thing possible to build up

muscle tone, probably better than most of my fancy and expensive machines!'

There wouldn't be another appointment in her treatment-rooms now until after New Year, and Kirsty was longing to get hold of the textbook and see what it said. But there was New Year to get through before she could do that, and a few people coming to celebrate it.

'I'd rather not have anyone,' Laura admitted to Kirsty, 'but I know Mark feels bad about leaving me. I'm sure Helen would rather go to some smart party—in fact it wouldn't surprise me at all if she's got something organised so that they come here and then move on.'

And that seemed to be the case, Kirsty thought on New Year's Eve, for she could see Mark and Helen having a—well, it was more than a discussion, it was closer to an argument, in one corner of the courtyard. Mark was shaking his head, and after a moment Helen shrugged and turned away. And Mark seemed to have won, because they were still there when the big bell outside the house was rung to tell everyone that New Year had come.

And at least this isn't too different from home, apart from the weather, Kirsty thought as one of Simon's friends kissed her and wished her a Happy New Year. She could see Mark kissing Helen—but not a very enthusiastic kiss, she found herself thinking—and then he came over and kissed Laura.

'Happy New Year, Kirsty,' he said then. There was something in his eyes that made her absurdly glad that she had worn the filmy sea-green dress Laura had insisted on lending her.

For a moment he hesitated, and then he kissed her. His lips were warm on hers, and as he kissed her someone moved behind him, pushing him even closer to her. Not that I mind at all, Kirsty thought, with honesty.

'Hey, Mark, move on—my turn with Kirsty!' Simon

said exuberantly. He took Kirsty in his arms, whirled her around, and kissed her. Watched by Mark, Kirsty knew.

As he set her down on her feet, Kirsty saw Helen coming across the room.

'Can we go now, Mark?' she said coolly. 'I had hoped we could move on to the van Zyls before midnight, but surely we can go now?'

'If you want to, Helen,' Mark said.

'Of course I want to—their parties are always such fun,' Helen said. She moved away, her silky blue dress moving smoothly with each step, her russet head high, and after a moment Mark followed her.

And I wonder what she will do if Mark is called out from this party? Kirsty thought uncharitably.

Which, as it turned out, he was, Laura told Kirsty later that day.

Kirsty had a momentary struggle with herself, and then she gave in and asked how Helen had taken that.

'Not very well, I gather,' Laura said. 'Mark didn't say much, but I did get that impression.'

The day after that was Laura's next physiotherapy treatment. Kirsty and Meg Russell talked about the daily sessions in the pool, and then Kirsty asked, casually, if she could borrow Meg's textbook while Laura had her treatment.

'Just something I want to check on,' she said.

She sat down in the small waiting-room and took out the notebook she had brought with her. She looked up the index, and found what she wanted. 'Psychosomatic interactions'. Quickly she skimmed through until she found what she was looking for. Yes, this was what she had half remembered—'a defence of the ego mechanism to handle anxiety, by producing physical symptoms'. Yes, that fits, she thought, forcing herself to write neatly, legibly. And then there was a comment that disturbances of sensation and motion were most common. She underlined that, when she had written it down.

And then, a little further down, she found the words she had half remembered. 'Disturbances of motion include paralysis, usually of the limbs.'

She wrote that down too, and then she closed the heavy book and put it back on the shelf.

Perhaps, she thought, if Laura had remained in Edinburgh, someone would have come up with this possibility. But they had only just finished excluding any physical cause, so there had been no time, no opportunity. And here she had only once seen the orthopaedic specialist.

'Disturbances of motion include paralysis'.

It made so much sense, following the accident—and earlier there had been a paragraph saying that a conversion reaction could develop after an organic illness had occurred. Or, Kirsty thought, an accident like a broken leg, an accident that removed the pressure of the problems Laura had wanted to get away from.

'Got all you need?' Meg Russell asked as she brought Laura through in her wheelchair.

'Yes, I have, thanks,' Kirsty replied.

For a moment she was tempted to take Laura to the car, and then to come back on the pretext of having forgotten something, to take the chance to talk to the physiotherapist, to ask her what she thought. But she knew that she couldn't do that; she had to talk to Mark first.

He didn't appear for dinner that night, and Laura said that he had mentioned that he and Helen were going out.

'Again?' Kirsty said involuntarily. 'Can she not see the poor man is tired, between his work and late calls and all this socialising?'

Laura's blue eyes met hers, a little surprised, and Kirsty found herself colouring up.

'Yes, I thought he looked tired, I must say,' she said. 'I don't know where they're going tonight, but he'll probably be late again.'

But Mark wasn't late.

Kirsty and Laura were sitting outside in the courtyard, both bathed and ready for bed, Kirsty wearing
a short cotton dressing-gown that Laura had lent her,
for her own dressing-gown was much too warm here.
Kirsty had just poured tea for them, when they heard
Mark's car draw up. It was some time, though, before
they heard the car door close, and then Mark's foot-
steps as he came through the house.

'You're early, Mark,' Laura said as he came through
the open door.

'Yes, I—suppose I am,' her brother replied after a
moment.

'Would you like some tea?' Kirsty asked. 'I'll get
another cup.' She stood up.

'No, wait a minute,' Mark said. For a moment his
eyes held hers, and then he turned to Laura. 'There's
something I want to tell you. Helen and I have broken
our engagement.'

CHAPTER TEN

WHAT should I say? Kirsty wondered, her thoughts whirling.

Laura, too, seemed to be having problems knowing how to react to what her brother had just said.

'Oh, Mark, I——' she began.

But before she could say any more, before Kirsty could even try to say something, the phone rang.

'Probably for me,' Mark said, and he turned and strode through the house. With some relief? Kirsty found herself wondering.

A few minutes later, he came to the open door to say that he had to go to see one of his patients in the clinic.

'Cholelithiasis,' he said briefly to Kirsty, and then to Laura, 'Gallstones. We've had her in for observation and it looks as if she'll have to be operated on pretty quickly.'

After he had gone, the two girls looked at each other.

'I suppose I should have said I was sorry,' Laura said at last, uncomfortably. 'But I couldn't honestly do that. More and more recently, I've been worried about how Helen would handle all the demands on Mark after they were married, if she found it hard now.'

Kirsty hesitated, telling herself that it really was none of her business. But Laura was looking at her, waiting for some comment.

'I must say I couldn't see Helen being very happy with Mark being on call as much as he is,' she said at last, with some reluctance. 'But she must have known before they got engaged what a GP's life is like?'

Laura shrugged.

115

'I think she was pretty certain she could persuade Mark to change that, to specialise,' she said.

Later, when Kirsty was in her room, alone, she found herself wondering, Had it been a mutual decision, to break their engagement? Or had Helen decided that if she wasn't going to be able to persuade Mark to become a specialist, then she wasn't interested in being the wife of a GP?

Or was it Mark who had broken the engagement?

And with that thought she had to admit to the question that had been in her mind all the time.

If this was Mark's decision, was it in any way because of her?

Immediately she was ashamed of the thought, for it was, she told herself, extremely presumptuous. And, she added, severely, highly unlikely!

But yet—that night, after they had swum, he had started to say something about Helen, and he had stopped. And then he had kissed her. And she had kissed him, she added to herself, fairly.

But after all, what was a kiss or two, once you accepted that there was a certain—physical attraction between two people? As she herself had said to Mark, a kiss was only a kiss, and no big deal.

And that is something you'd better remember, my girl, she told herself.

The next morning, Mark was coming out of his room, obviously on his way to work, when Kirsty was on her way to the breakfast-room to get some orange juice to take to Laura. And, because she had spoken to herself pretty sternly, she was able to say, 'Mark, I'm sorry about you and Helen.'

He looked down at her.

'I think we've both known for some time it wasn't going to work, Kirsty,' he said slowly. 'We just both had to admit that.'

It wasn't, Kirsty knew, the right time to say anything to him of her thoughts about Laura, and to tell him what she had read about possible reactions in psychosomatic illnesses. Perhaps tonight she would get the chance.

Instead she asked him about his gallstone patient.

'The gallstone had gone right through the cystic duct, so it wasn't too easy an operation,' he told her. 'But Bob Matthews is the best man for this sort of thing—he did a ligation of the cystic duct and artery, and did it beautifully; it was a privilege to be assisting him. No, she'll do all right now, thanks, although of course we'll keep her in for about ten days.'

Yes, Kirsty thought as he walked through the big *voorkamer* to the door, we are probably safer talking about your gallstone lady, Mark, rather than your broken engagement, or your sister being unable to walk.

Laura's friend Jan came through from Cape Town in the afternoon, in time to join Laura and Kirsty for Laura's short session in the swimming-pool. This was the first time anyone else had been around when Laura was in the pool, and Kirsty was glad of Jan's matter-of-fact approach.

Yes, she said, she'd heard that any exercises done in the water were more effective, because of the body working against the pressure of the water. Kirsty, gently moving Laura's legs in the water as the phsyiotherapist had taught her, looked up at the girl sitting on the edge, and agreed.

'Gosh, Kirsty, Laura's lucky having you to do this and the massage and her other exercises with her,' Jan said.

'Any trained nurse could learn to do that,' Kirsty assured her, with truth. 'And the exercises are really simple—you wouldn't even have to be a nurse to be able to learn how to do them.'

She helped Laura out of the water and into the wheelchair, well wrapped in a big towel, and they went back into the cool of the house, and through to Laura's room.

Mark wasn't home for dinner, and Laura told Sarah

they'd like to have cold chicken and salad outside, in
the small courtyard.

'And pudding?' Sarah said hopefully. 'I could make
nice *pannekoek* for you.'

'No pancakes, thank you,' Laura said firmly. 'Just
some fruit.'

With an elaborate sigh, and muttering something
under her breath, Sarah went back to her kitchen.

It was an easy and relaxed meal, but Kirsty was once
again conscious that although she was only two or three
years older than Laura and Jan there did seem to be
more of a gap than those actual years. Perhaps you
did grow up faster when you did something like nursing, she thought. It wasn't, she thought, that she felt
old compared to them; she just felt that she'd—grown
up a bit more, perhaps.

Laura and Jan went to play Scrabble in Laura's
room, when they had finished eating, and Kirsty,
enjoying the pleasant cool of the evening—well, she
thought, cool compared with the heat of the day—took
her mother's letter outside to reply to.

It was perhaps just as well, she thought, that the
airmail form wasn't very big, for there really wasn't a
great deal to tell her folks, in terms of what she had
been doing. Taking Laura for her phsyiotherapy treatment, going for walks around the farm, how the baby
she had delivered, Sarah Kirsty, was doing.

'Your Hogmanay and New Year sounded great,' she
wrote. 'They don't call it Hogmanay here, it's Old
Year's Eve, but folks still kiss each other and say
Happy New Year, just the same, when the bells ring.'

She paused, the pen in her hand, and only space for
a line or two. 'I miss you all,' she wrote. 'Love, Kirsty.'

And she realised, as she wrote it, just how true it
was. She did miss them all—Mum, Dad, Gavin, Gran.
Much more than she had expected to, when she had
set out so light-heartedly, glad of the chance to travel,
to see something more of the world.

'Tears again, Kirsty?' Mark said, beside her.

'Just a wee tear,' Kirsty replied quickly, defensively, and she brushed the back of her hand across her eyes. 'It was just—I was writing to my mum, and I said, I miss you all, and—and it sort of hit me that I did.'

He sat down on the cane couch beside her.

'You're a nice girl, Kirsty Cameron,' he said, taking her by surprise. 'Funny, when I first met you, I thought——'

He stopped.

'What did you think?' she asked him, although she was pretty sure she knew.

He smiled, a slow, warm smile that did very strange things to her.

'Oh, I thought you were—flighty, irresponsible, much too independent. And too much given to interfering in things you knew nothing about.'

He leaned back against the big cushions of the couch, and turned his head to look at her.

'I'm sorry, but you did ask,' he said.

'Oh, I don't mind,' Kirsty assured him, with truth. 'Because I had you taped too. Arrogant, bossy, selfish.'

Somehow he seemed to have moved closer to her.

'And now?' he asked, his voice low. 'Do you still think I'm all that?'

'Not all of it,' Kirsty returned. 'Maybe a wee bit bossy, though.'

Mark laughed, his dark head thrown back.

'You're actually a "wee bit bossy" yourself, Kirsty,' he said.

His lips were warm on hers, warm and gentle, and then not at all gentle, but demanding and searching. Even if she had wanted to, Kirsty could have done nothing but respond to the urgent demand of his lips, his hands.

Slowly, with reluctance, he drew back. She could hear his uneven breathing, so close to her—or was it her own uneven breathing?

'Look, Kirsty, I have to say this,' he said, not quite steadily. 'Helen and I agreed that we both felt the best

thing to do was to break our engagement, and that's
what we've told people, because it's true. But a girl
like Helen has her pride. I owe it to her to—well,
to let her be the first one to show an interest in
someone else.'

His voice was steady now, but he was carefully not
touching her. His eyes, as he looked down at her, were
very dark.

'You do understand what I'm saying, Kirsty?'
he asked.

'Yes,' Kirsty said simply. 'You're telling me that
after Helen finds someone else you'll be free to—be
free to——'

Her directness left her then, and her voice faltered.

'Go on, Kirsty,' Mark said, and there was warm
teasing in his voice.

Kirsty shook her head.

'No,' she said, 'I'm not going to say any more!'

'As long as you understand,' he murmured.

I think I do, Kirsty thought, wonderingly, when he
had gone. It was pretty clear, after all. Pretty clear,
and so unbelievable that she dared not let herself dwell
on it. Or on how she would feel if—if she had understood him correctly, if he really meant what she
thought he meant.

And oh, dear, Kirsty thought ruefully, here I am so
thrown by this that I didn't take the chance to talk to
him about Laura.

And of course, she reminded herself soberly, it could
take some time for Helen to start seeing someone else.
Although surely not, she being so beautiful, and so
elegant, and always looking so perfect?

It was a strange feeling, through the next two days,
she thought, almost as if she were two people. The one
Kirsty functioned perfectly adequately and practically,
doing Laura's massage, and her exercises, taking her
for her physiotherapy treatment, becoming more and
more skilled and at ease using the laser, talking to
Sarah, going to visit Zita and her baby, taking Rufus

for a walk, meeting Simon on the way back.

That was the Kirsty she had always prided herself on being.

But the other Kirsty was in a dream, remembering what Mark had said, remembering the way he had looked at her, remembering how she had felt in his arms.

Mark didn't come home till late that evening, too late for her to wait up to talk to him about Laura. He was at a lecture at University in Cape Town, Laura told her.

Laura hadn't mentioned Jonathan again since the day they had met him in Stellenbosch. Kirsty didn't think it would be wise to force her into any confidences she wasn't really ready to share yet, but she had an instinctive feeling that, since this was part of the problem, the sooner Laura faced up to it, and brought it all out into the open, the better.

But I'm out of my depth, with this, Kirsty reminded herself, until I talk to Mark, and we decide what we should do about it all.

The next night, after she had helped Laura to bed, she went outside, waiting for the chance to talk to Mark. He had been a little abstracted at dinner, she thought, although he had talked about the lecture on genetic counselling he had gone to.

And he had told them that the south-easter was blowing strongly in Cape Town, and there shouldn't be the danger of rain inland to put at risk the ripening fields of grapes.

'The south-easter is called the Cape Doctor, Kirsty,' he'd said, 'because it blows all the germs and all the illnesses away. They can't run the cableway when it's too strong, of course.'

'Mark, you really must take Kirsty, up the mountain,' Laura had said then. 'It's incredible, Kirsty, to be on the top of Table Mountain looking down at the whole of the Peninsula spread out below. Actually, you have to see it by day, and then you should go up

Signal Hill at night, and see all the lights.'

She had turned to her brother.

'Do take Kirsty through, Mark; there's so much she should see in Cape Town.'

For a moment Mark's eyes had met Kirsty's.

'Good idea,' he'd said. 'We'll all go.'

Laura had shaken her head.

'No, you take Kirsty—I've been often enough, and besides——' She'd lifted her chin. 'Besides,' she'd said levelly, 'it wouldn't be very easy to take a wheelchair in the cable car, and over the top of Table Mountain, now would it?'

Mark and Kirsty had exchanged glances, and then he'd agreed that it could be difficult to have a wheelchair on the mountain.

Kirsty was thinking of that as she waited for Mark in the warm darkness of the summer night. I will be very glad, she thought soberly, to share all this with Mark, because maybe it's counselling or therapy Laura will need, and I'm out of my depth.

She knew that Mark always checked on all the doors last thing, and it was after eleven. Was that him coming now?

'Mark?' she said.

He came out to the courtyard.

'Kirsty? I didn't know you were there.'

'I was waiting for you,' she said. 'I have to talk to you, Mark.'

He didn't move.

'Don't make things too difficult for me—for us,' he said after a moment.

'No,' Kirsty said, startled. 'No, I wasn't—it's about Laura.'

He sat down, but on the chair, not on the couch beside her.

Kirsty took a deep breath, and began. She told him that she had begun to think about things Laura had said. That it was all too much for her. And that going away hadn't seemed a bad idea.

And Jonathan Payne saying, 'I guess it all got too much for her to handle'.

She went on quickly after that, conscious of Mark stiffening at the mention of the young artist.

'The words I was thinking about were hysterical paralysis,' she said. 'And when I looked it up it makes sense, Mark. Listen to this.'

She took out her notebook and read out to him some of the things she had copied out. The light above the small table was dim, but she almost knew the words off by heart anyway.

'"Disturbances of sensation and motion are most common,"' she read aloud. 'And this, Mark. "Disturbances of motion include paralysis, usually of the limbs."'

She put her notebook down on the table and looked at him.

It was a little while before he spoke.

'So,' he said at last, 'Laura's condition defeated the experts in the Edinburgh hospital, but you've managed to solve it. Clever girl, Kirsty.'

There was something in his voice—he must be blaming the Edinburgh team for not thinking of this, Kirsty told herself.

She leaned forward.

'They didn't really have time, Mark,' she pointed out. 'The last of Laura's tests was only just finished before we came away. I'm sure if she had been there longer they would have thought of this. And your Dr Brown here—he's only seen her once; he would probably have come to this conclusion too, when he saw her again. It's just with me being with Laura all the time, getting to know her, I began to wonder.'

'Ah, yes, and after wondering you checked,' Mark said. 'Where did you get hold of a textbook?'

'I borrowed one of Meg Russell's, last time Laura was having phsyiotherapy,' Kirsty told him. 'I didn't say anything to Meg; I wanted to tell you first. But it all fits perfectly, doesn't it, Mark?'

He was silent for a long time. Too long, she began to realise.

'Do you know what you're saying?' he said at last, and his voice was dangerously quiet. 'You are telling me that I am to blame for my sister being in a wheelchair. Aren't you?'

Bewildered, completely thrown—not only by what he was saying but by the way he was saying it—Kirsty was unable to reply for a moment or two.

'I—suppose I am,' she said finally, with difficulty.

'What nonsense!' Mark said. 'Do you really think Laura is so afraid of me that she has to take refuge in that damned wheelchair?'

Slowly the shock of his unexpected reaction was passing. Kirsty tried to control her rising anger.

'I don't think it's nonsense,' she returned, and she managed to keep her voice steady. 'It seems to me that for a girl like Laura, accustomed to doing what her brother wanted, it provided an answer, a way out. And anyway it was all unconscious; she wasn't taking a decision to do this.'

'Don't be ridiculous,' Mark said. And worse than his anger was the cold hostility in his voice.

He stood up then, and walked over to the low wall, standing with his back to her. Kirsty's chin rose.

'What is your explanation, then?' she said.

'Post-accident trauma,' he said brusquely, without turning round. 'She needs time, that's all.'

The only thing that mattered, really, was Laura, Kirsty reminded herself.

She stood up too.

'She's had plenty of time,' she pointed out. 'She needs to know that there are no pressures; she needs to know that she is free to live her own life.'

'With a penniless artist, in a rented cottage?' Mark asked scornfully.

'If that's what Laura wants, then yes,' Kirsty returned.

Mark swung round.

'Do you really think,' he said, not quite steadily, 'that when Laura hears this ridiculous theory she will get out of that wheelchair and walk?'

'No, I don't think that,' Kirsty replied. 'Perhaps she'll need counselling, or therapy, I don't know. I thought that was something we could talk about.'

'"We"?' he said, throwing the word back at her. 'There is no "we" in this, Kirsty. I cannot go along with this ridiculous idea that could do no more than give Laura false hope; that would be cruel.'

Afterwards, Kirsty knew that it would have been wiser to think before she spoke.

'You're the one who is cruel, Mark,' she said shakily.

She knew, as soon as she had said it, that she had gone too far.

In the dim light of the courtyard, Mark looked down at her. 'That is unforgivable,' he said.

And Kirsty, her heart sinking, knew that it was. But it was too late; the words were said.

'I don't want to hear another word about this,' he said then. 'And I want you to promise me you will say nothing to Laura.'

Kirsty was silent.

'Remember, you are in my employ,' Mark said brusquely.

And that was as unforgivable as anything she had said to him, Kirsty thought. There was only one possible reply to that.

'Then perhaps we had better put an end to that,' she said, her voice as cool as his had been. 'Perhaps I had better leave.'

CHAPTER ELEVEN

ANGRY as he was, Mark knew that he should not have said what he had. But the last thing he could do right now was to take it back.

He looked down at Kirsty, her hazel eyes furious in her white face.

'Leave?' he repeated. 'You can't do that. Laura needs you.'

'I don't see how I can stay,' Kirsty replied, and he could see that she was fighting to keep her voice steady.

The unforgivable, unthinkable things she had said, this ridiculous suggestion that Laura's only defence against him had been to find that she couldn't walk— yes, he thought, perhaps it would be better if she left.

But he knew he could not let that happen, because of Laura.

'You once said you wouldn't go back on your word,' he reminded her. 'But that's what you're doing now. You can't walk out on Laura.'

It was a long time before she replied.

'I'll stay,' she said at last, quietly. 'And you won't have to remind me again that I'm in your employ. I'm not likely to forget it.'

She turned then and walked away from him, back into the house. And Mark, watching her go, was still so full of anger and resentment at the things she had suggested that there was no room for any regrets, no room even for any fleeting memories of the way he had felt when he'd held this girl in his arms.

And he would not, he told himself the next day, give Kirsty Cameron or the ridiculous things she had said another thought. And fortunately his waiting-room was always so busy, his list of patients to see so long, that there was no time to think of anything else. There was an outbreak of flu, a summer flu that could sometimes hit harder than a winter flu, and half a dozen cases of chickenpox at the local schools.

And he had promised his mother's old friend, Esther Wingate, that he would be there when she had her angiogram.

'Only as an observor, you realise,' he reminded her as she was wheeled into the small theatre where the huge machine was. She nodded, and he was glad he had made himself find the time to come, because he could see the apprehension in her eyes as she lay on the trolley. The procedure could not be done under general anaesthetic because the patient had to be conscious to co-operate, but she had been given a sedative.

Mark, capped and gowned and booted, was given a position where Esther Wingate could see him, but he wasn't in the way of the small and efficient theatre team. The huge camera was positioned above her, and the cardiologist told her that he was going to make a small groin incision, and insert the dye.

'You might feel a slightly unpleasant sensation as it goes into your veins,' he said. 'I'm controlling it all the way, and from time to time I'll ask you to take a deep breath, so that we can take a still.' Briefly, he glanced over at Mark. 'Good—you can see Dr Barnard, and he can see the monitor.'

The monitor itself was so fascinating that Mark would have liked to watch it all the time, but he kept glancing at his patient, and once or twice, when she looked a little distressed, he smiled reassuringly.

The smooth efficiency of the theatre team impressed him, as it always did.

'Deep breath, Mrs Wingate,' the specialist said, and Mrs Wingate, her eyes on Mark's face, did what she was told.

Once, when a still picture was wanted, Mark glanced at the screen, and he saw an obstruction in the vein, an obstruction that would of course show up more clearly on the still picture.

The whole procedure took some time, and when it

was over the theatre sister took Mrs Wingate back to
the ward, where she would have to spend the rest of
the day lying completely still.

'I'm glad you were here, Mark,' she said as she was
wheeled out.

'So am I,' Mark replied, meaning it.

'I'll give you a ring later, Mark, when we get these
stills developed,' the specialist said. 'And we can discuss anything further.'

Interesting, Mark thought as he went back to his
rooms, but I'm still happier being a GP. He glanced
at the full waiting-room and added ruefully to himself,
Even if it will be late before I get this lot clear!

In the days following, Mark was scrupulously polite to
Kirsty, and she was equally polite to him. Sometimes
she would find Laura's eyes resting on her, and then
moving to Mark, questioning. But she was grateful that
Laura didn't say anything to her, for it would have
been difficult to conceal the anger and the resentment
she felt. And impossible to explain the reasons.

And then, slowly, the anger seeped away, and pain
and bewilderment took its place. How could Mark have
spoken to her like that, how could be have looked at
her like that, after the way things had been between
them? When she closed her eyes at night, she could
remember his arms around her, his lips close to hers,
she could remember the warm teasing in his voice, she
could remember the promise in what he had said.

But now all that was gone. Gone because of what
she had said, because he wouldn't accept that his attitude could have anything to do with the refuge that
Laura's unconscious mind had made her take.

And yet, Kirsty thought, more than once, I couldn't
have done anything else, and I would do it over again,
even knowing what it would lead to, knowing what I
would lose. I would have to.

She didn't know what she would do now.

She hadn't, in fact, made Mark the promise he had

asked of her, the promise not to talk about this to
Laura. But she knew that she could not do that. She
was out of her depth, and it could be distressing, perhaps even dangerous, for someone inexperienced to
confront Laura in that way.

No, she couldn't say anything to Laura. But she had
to talk to someone.

Meg Russell, the phsyiotherapist, she thought. Meg
was professionally involved, she was practical, and she
was clear-sighted.

On the pretext of some shopping she needed to do,
Kirsty drove into Stellenbosch one afternoon when Jan
was at Bloemenkloof visiting Laura. The phsyiotherapist was busy, but when Kirsty said she wanted to talk
to her Meg said that she had a cancelled appointment
in half an hour, if Kirsty could wait.

'Right,' Meg said briskly as she closed the door on
her patient some thirty minutes later. 'My receptionist
is glad to have half an hour off, so we're on our own.
Sugar with your coffee? No, I didn't think so. What's
the problem?'

Kirsty took a sip of her coffee, and then set the mug
down. Slowly at first, and then with more confidence,
she told the older woman her thoughts, and then what
she had found in the textbook.

'I wondered what it was you wanted to look up,'
Meg said.

She stood up then, and lifted the heavy book down
from the shelf. Swiftly, she read the page Kirsty had
mentioned, and then she put the book down on her
desk, still open.

'I must say it did cross my mind that this just might
be psychosomatic,' she said. 'I hadn't got much beyond
that thought, but it makes sense. I didn't know Laura
had had these problems, of course. This isn't something I've come across, so I don't know the answer.
Mark should know what to do—you'll talk to him
right away?'

'I already have,' Kirsty said bleakly. 'He won't even

consider it as a possibility; he thinks I'm talking nonsense.' And then, because some strange and unexpected protectiveness—loyalty? She wasn't sure what—came over her, she said carefully that she should have realised Mark might take it personally, inferring that he was the cause of Laura's paralysis.

'It isn't only him, of course, there's Jonathan, too,' Kirsty said. 'But I didn't get the chance to say that to Mark.'

The physiotherapist considered that.

'Well,' she said at last, a little unconvincingly, 'perhaps now that you have suggested it Mark will think about it and see that it's a real possibility.'

Kirsty shook her head.

'I doubt it,' she said with feeling.

'Want me to try talking to him?' Meg suggested, but Kirsty said she thought not, at the moment. Mark would certainly know she had talked to Meg, if that happened, and that wouldn't be a good idea.

'Let me think about it,' Kirsty said, rising as Meg's next patient knocked at the door and came in. 'It's been a help just talking to you.'

And that, she thought, was true. Somehow, after the way Mark had reacted, she had lost confidence in her own thinking, but talking to Meg had restored that, had made her realise that she was right to feel that this could be the answer.

It was late afternoon when she got back, and the heat of the day had gone. Laura's friend Jan had already left for Cape Town.

'Could we go for a walk?' Laura asked, and Kirsty agreed, glad to have Laura suggest doing something, rather than just agree with whatever she herself suggested.

She pushed the wheelchair through the vineyards, where the workers were finishing for the day, their voices loud in the still air. Rufus ran ahead of them, and when they reached the little river Kirsty whistled for him, ready to turn back.

'No,' Laura said suddenly. 'Let's go over the bridge
and into the wood on the other side. It—it's nice there,
and the path is quite smooth.'

And after that? Kirsty wondered. Would Laura want
to turn back, once they were over on the other side?

But Laura, it seemed, had come to a decision.

'Kirsty,' she said quietly, 'I'd like to go to the
cottage, to see Jonathan.'

Kirsty looked down at her.

'You're sure you want to do that?' she asked.

Laura nodded.

'Yes, I'm sure,' she replied. 'I—I've been thinking
about it since we met Jonathan that day.'

Still Kirsty hesitated.

'And Mark?' she said at last, carefully.

Laura's chin rose.

'I'll deal with Mark,' she said. 'Anyway. . .' For a
moment Kirsty thought Laura was going to say something more, then she shrugged. 'Don't worry, Kirsty,'
she said then quietly. 'I have thought about this, and
I do want to do it, and I take full responsibility for it.'

The path on the other side of the river was wide at
first, going through the wood, and quite smooth, but
as it wound its way deeper it became steeper, and there
were tree roots that made it difficult for the wheelchair.

With the cottage in sight, Kirsty stopped, uncertain
whether she could manage this last steep slope.

'I'm sorry, Kirsty,' Laura said. 'I hadn't realised it
was so steep. Perhaps we'd better turn.'

Kirsty shook her head.

'Not at this stage,' she said, and she knew that
she meant more than just this stage of the path
through the wood. She whistled for Rufus then,
uncertain whether he was ahead or behind, and he
reappeared—followed by Jonathan Payne.

'Rufus came to tell me I had visitors,' he said. 'Let
me give you a hand, Kirsty.'

But when he put his hands on the wheelchair Laura's
courage and her certainty seemed to disappear.

'No,' she said. 'I don't want you pushing my wheel-chair, Jonathan.'

Jonathan, his brown, paint-spattered hands steady on the chair, looked down at her.

'Why not? The path is steep, Kirsty can't manage, and I'm here,' he pointed out reasonably. And then he said, his voice gentle, 'Laura, let's not be foolish. We can't behave as if you're not in a wheelchair, because you are. I just want to say one thing. If something like this had happened to me, wouldn't you push my wheelchair? Think about that, Laura.'

Then, his hands strong and capable, he pushed the wheelchair the rest of the way to the cottage.

'Get the mugs out, will you, Laura? I'll put the kettle on,' he said when they were inside. 'You know where everything is.'

Kirsty, on the point of stepping in, stopped herself. A little awkwardly, Laura manoeuvred her wheelchair over to a big cupboard, and got out three bright mugs and a tin with biscuits in it. Then, with the mugs and the tin on her lap, she made her way back to the table.

'Thanks,' Jonathan said, his voice casual. But not, Kirsty saw, his eyes as they rested on the fair-haired girl in the wheelchair.

'I'll go for a walk,' she said when she had finished her mug of tea. 'Come on, Rufus. But we can't be long, Laura; it's getting late.'

Half an hour later, when she got back to the cottage, Laura and Jonathan were outside, Jonathan sitting on a grassy bank beside Laura's wheelchair.

'I did suggest setting Laura down on the grass, but she feels safer in her chair,' he said. There was something buoyant in his voice, in his eyes that made Kirsty look at Laura carefully, and see that there was colour in her cheeks and a brightness in her eyes that hadn't been there before. But there was still, when Laura looked at the young artist, a troubled look about her, and Kirsty saw that Jonathan too was far from any real confidence and certainty.

Laura said little about their visit on the way home, other than to thank Kirsty, and to say that she would like to go back again in a few days. But she was very thoughtful, Kirsty noticed, and in a different way from before, when Kirsty had often seen her sitting silent, her hands clasped, looking unseeingly out of the window.

Now she would sit quietly, but somehow the sadness and the distance were less evident. Not gone, but now there was something more positive, more hopeful about Laura. She looks, Kirsty thought, as if she's doing an awful lot of thinking.

She did, though, ask Kirsty if she and Mark had quarrelled.

'Why do you ask?' Kirsty said quickly—too quickly, too defensively, she knew.

Laura smiled, but her blue eyes were concerned.

'Oh, Kirsty,' she said, 'anyone could see that the two of you are distinctly cool with each other. You hardly ever address each other directly, and when you have to you say as little as possible.'

Kirsty shrugged.

'Och, we've never been what you might call great buddies, your brother and I,' she said, as lightly as she was able to. 'You know that, Laura.'

'Yes, but you seemed to be getting on quite well together recently,' Laura said.

'Don't worry,' Kirsty said then. 'Any problem between Mark and me doesn't have to bother you.'

But Laura wasn't giving up that easily.

'I know you think Mark is a bit arrogant, a bit too sure of himself,' she said slowly, 'and you're probably right, but he had to take charge of the farm, and the house, and me, when our folks died. And he's having a tough time just now, between worry about me and his broken engagement. I wonder if he knows that Helen is seeing Brent Conran? Jan was telling me they were at a big charity ball together.'

Afterwards, when she was alone, Kirsty could allow

herself to think about that. To think, sadly, that for a short time she had been hoping so much for something like this. Now it didn't make any difference.

Most of the time, she was still so angry and hurt at Mark's reaction that there was no room for any other emotion. But sometimes, late at night, when the house was still, she would sit at her open window in the warm darkness and she would wipe a silent tear away.

You're a foolish girl, she told herself severely, wasting your tears on a man like him. Because all the things she had thought of him were perfectly true, she reminded herself. He was arrogant, he was bossy and too sure of himself. All right, as Laura had pointed out, there were good enough reasons for that; maybe he'd had to become that way. But it had all made him an awful difficult man to live with—to be around, she corrected herself hastily. And it had been quite unforgivable, his telling her that she was in his employ.

I told him I wouldn't forget that again, and I certainly won't, she said to herself. It's a fine, straightforward relationship, and there's no room for any misunderstandings in it; we both know just where we stand.

In spite of all that had happened between Mark and her, Kirsty found that she was beginning to feel part of the life here at Bloemenkloof. Sarah treated her much as she did Laura, reprimanding her when she didn't eat as much as Sarah thought she should, telling her sternly that she wasn't getting enough sleep. Simon's easy friendship she found very heart-warming. She looked in regularly to see young Zita and baby Sarah Kirsty. The farm workers all greeted her when she took Rufus for a walk. And she was getting to know the children in the crèche.

Most days, Laura spent some time working on the books and the study papers Jan had brought her, and when it was too hot to walk or to swim Kirsty would go to the crèche. At first she just sat and watched what the teacher, Aletta Johnson, was doing, but gradually

she began to join in, and soon the children would
demand that Nurse Kirsty join in any games, or help
them with colouring-in, or read a story to them.

'I like the way you speak, Nurse Kirsty,' small, red-
haired Andrew said to her one day, in the middle of
The Cat in the Hat. 'My granny speaks just like you;
she came to us for a holiday, but now she's gone far,
far away. But you speak just like her, and I told my
mummy it's nice when you come.'

'Thank you, Andrew,' Kirsty said gravely. 'I'm glad
you like the way I speak.'

'I like it too, Nurse Kirsty,' Thandi assured her,
determined not to be left out. And then said truthfully,
'But my gran doesn't speak like you.'

Kirsty hugged the small girl.

'No, I don't suppose she does,' she agreed.

And suddenly she was conscious of being watched.
She looked up, and Mark was standing at the door.
Just as she herself had stood, that first time she had
seen him here with the children.

Awkwardly, she scrambled to her feet.

'Aletta will be back in a minute,' she said defensively. 'She just went to make a phone call.'

'I finished early, so I thought I might as well take
the chance to look in on the children,' Mark said, just
as defensively. 'I didn't know you would be here.'

The implication being, Kirsty knew, that if he had
he wouldn't have come.

'I was just going,' she said.

Thandi's small hand clutched hers.

'You must stay, Nurse Kirsty,' she said imperiously.
'Dr Mark is going to look at my sroat to see if I can
go to hostipal.'

Kirsty found she had to struggle to maintain her
gravity as she sorted out the little girl's words, and
came to throat and hospital.

'Do stay,' Mark said stiffly. 'I can see the children
like having you here. Now, Thandi, let me have a look
at that throat of yours. Say ah for me.'

He pressed the tongue depressor gently on the little girl's tongue.

'That looks better,' he said with satisfaction, and he turned to Kirsty. 'Thandi has had tonsil problems for months, but we were trying to hold out until she was three. Then she got another infection, but they seem to be settled now; I'll let them know at the hospital.'

'I'm going to hostipal,' Thandi said importantly to Andrew. 'And you're not, just me.'

For a moment, above the small black head and the small red head, Mark's eyes met Kirsty's. Just one moment of shared warmth and amusement, and then the curtain of coldness was back again. And on my side just as much as his, Kirsty knew.

She didn't want to have to walk back to the house with Mark, but the children wouldn't let her go until Mark had checked over them all. Their teacher, Mrs Johnson, returned just as Mark finished.

'Sorry,' she said breathlessly, 'it took longer than I thought. I'm so glad you were here.' She turned to Mark. 'Kirsty is such a help; most days she looks in, and the children so much enjoy having her here.'

And I had better sort that out, Kirsty thought as Mark's eyes met hers.

There was no option now but to walk back to the house together, but as soon as they were outside she told him that she only came here when Laura was doing some studying.

'That's quite all right,' Mark replied, his voice as polite as hers. 'You are entitled to time off. I appreciate your choosing to spend some of it with the children.'

'Not at all,' Kirsty said. 'I love being with them.'

Mark said then that he thought it looked like rain, and he hoped not, for the sake of the grapes, at this stage. Kirsty said yes, she had been interested to learn how much of a problem rain could be, if it came at the wrong time.

We're like strangers, she thought sadly. Strangers

who don't have much in common, and who don't really like each other very much.

Just as they reached the house, Mark stopped.

'Kirsty. . .' he said.

She stopped too.

'Yes?' she said, very carefully.

He hesitated.

'I was thinking—perhaps you could visit Thandi when she's in hospital; I'm sure she would appreciate that.'

'Yes, I'll do that,' Kirsty agreed.

But she had the strange, troubling certainty that that was not what Mark had set out to say to her.

Laura was waiting for them on the *stoep*, a tray with tea beside her. Kirsty hurried forward to pour the tea, but Laura shook her head.

'I'll do it,' she said.

She handed a cup to Kirsty, and another to Mark. Then she looked up at her brother.

'It's only a few days till my birthday, Mark,' she reminded him. 'I know we said we'd let it be a surprise for Kirsty, but I can't wait; I'm going to tell her now, so that she has time to look forward to it.'

'Laura. . .' Mark began, obviously thrown by this. 'Maybe you and I should discuss this first.'

Laura shook her head.

'We've already discussed it—we made all the plans before Christmas.'

Plans? Kirsty wondered. And look forward? Surely Laura wasn't wanting to have a birthday party, and her still unwilling to go out in public in her wheelchair?

'A birthday party, Laura?' she asked.

'Oh, no, much better than that,' Laura replied. She set her cup down. 'We have a friend who has a private game reserve,' she said. 'Well, he's a friend now, but he started off as a grateful patient of Mark's; he was on holiday in Stellenbosch, and he had—what was it, Mark?'

'A perforated ulcer,' Mark said. 'Laura, I——'

But Laura, for once, was not the usual obedient
young sister. She swept on.

'Well, he says Mark saved his life, and since then
we've gone to Malalozi quite often. It's the most marvellous place, Kirsty, and this is a quiet time of year,
and I love it so much that I don't even mind that I
won't be able to do—to do all the things I used to.
Just to be there will be marvellous. We're going there
for my birthday, for a few days, just the three of us.
You and Mark and I.'

'Just the three of us,' Kirsty echoed bleakly.

And she saw her own dismay mirrored in
Mark's eyes.

CHAPTER TWELVE

'Yes, just the three of us,' Laura said.

She seemed oblivious to the lack of enthusiasm from both Mark and Kirsty as she told Kirsty that they would travel to the game park in a private plane.

'And flying in like that is incredible. Sometimes you see herds of springbok, or impala, or kudu. We saw giraffes from the air once. Remember, Mark?'

Mark nodded.

'Yes, I remember. Look, Laura—I'm not so sure I should be taking time off right now. And it's the height of summer; we probably wouldn't see much game. Maybe we should wait a bit.'

'Oh, Mark,' Laura said, her disappointment all too obvious, 'you promised. I've been looking forward so much to showing Kirsty the bushveld.' She looked away, but not before Kirsty had seen that she was close to tears. 'And to getting back to Malalozi myself.' Her voice was low.

Mark sighed.

'Right, then, I'll organise a locum, and I'll ring Jake and find out when he can send the plane for us. You'll keep Kirsty right on what she should take?'

I'm right here in the room, Kirsty thought with resentment. You don't have to speak as if I'm somewhere else!

When he had gone, Laura looked at Kirsty.

'I don't usually do that sort of thing,' she said, a little awkwardly. 'The emotional blackmail line, I mean.'

'I must say I was a little surprised,' Kirsty admitted. 'Does it mean so much to you, Laura, going to this place?'

'It does mean a lot to me,' Laura said slowly. She looked down at her useless legs. 'Sometimes, after this happened, I used to think about being at Malalozi, think about the bushveld in the morning, with the red in the sky, a real African sunrise. Or the quietness at night, when you're in the camp. And lately I've been sort of counting on getting there; I have this feeling that it will help me to get myself together, somehow. Ready to face up to—to anything.'

Kirsty covered Laura's clasped hands with her own for a moment.

'Then I'm all for us going there,' she said, not quite steadily.

'But Mark needs it too,' Laura said then. 'Kirsty, I know the two of you don't hit it off, but he's my brother, and I love him dearly, and—you may find this hard to believe, but I do worry about him sometimes. It's funny, but right after he and Helen broke up I wasn't worried at all; I couldn't help thinking it was the best thing for Mark—probably for Helen too. But somehow that didn't last. He's very tense, very withdrawn. I really think it will do him the world of good to have a few days at Malalozi.'

She smiled, her blue eyes warm.

'And you too, Kirsty; I know you'll love it. Let's go through to your room and check over your clothes.'

Jeans and T-shirts, it seemed, would do for anything, and good stout shoes.

'And, of course, we'll be swimming, so take your costume,' Laura said. She lifted her chin. 'I'll take mine too—this should be a quiet time in the camp, and it would be a pity for me to miss my hydrotherapy.'

And that is brave of Laura, Kirsty thought, even to think about going into the water when there might be other people around.

Three days later, Simon drove them to the airport, where the small plane was ready for them.

'Jake de Villiers usually flies his plane himself,' Mark said as they went across to the plane. 'But he has a pilot on stand-by, and right now he couldn't get away himself.'

'He's a cattle farmer as well as owning the game park,' Laura said. Her cheeks were pink with excitement when Mark carried her into the small plane, and she peered out of the window to watch Simon and Mark lifting her wheelchair up.

'Have fun,' Simon said, coming up into the cabin. He bent and kissed Laura, and then Kirsty. And Kirsty's kiss was very clearly considerably more intimate than the cousinly one he had given Laura. Kirsty, determinedly freeing herself, found Mark's eyes on her, dark, remote.

'See you when you get back,' Simon said, unrepentant.

The game farm was in the Western Transvaal.

'Not far from Sun City,' Laura said, peering out as they approached the landing strip a few hours later. 'And Lost City, of course. Mark, you should take Kirsty over to see Lost City one night; it sounds as if it's really something.'

'No,' Mark said, quite rudely. And then, as if realising this, he said to Kirsty, 'If you look out now, Kirsty, you'll see the crater of the extinct volcano. The game park is right in the heart of it. We're too high still to see any game, but—no, look, a herd of zebras, over to the right.'

Kirsty peered out. There were the zebras and, beyond them, something else.

'Buck of some kind,' Mark said. 'Probably kudu.'

Kirsty was all too conscious of how close to her he was as they looked out of the small window. Once, his cheek touched hers, and it was just a little rough. She couldn't help remembering that first time, in the plane coming over, when she had wakened to find her head on his shoulder, and had felt the roughness of his face close to hers.

She moved away, and at the same moment so did Mark.

The owner of the game park, Mark's ex-patient, Jake de Villiers, wasn't able to leave his farm, but he

had left a small Suzuki estate van for them to use, the
head game ranger told them when they landed. And
the guest cottage was ready for them.

The guest cottage was brick, with a thatched roof,
and although there were half a dozen other similar
cottages each one was built to ensure privacy. Inside
it was cool and pleasant, with a large living area,
including a kitchen with, Kirsty saw, a microwave
oven, a small cooker and a large fridge. There was a
bedroom on each side, each with its own bathroom.
Laura and Kirsty were to share one room, and Mark
would have the other.

'And Jake has organised all sorts of food ready for
us—he always does,' Laura said, adroitly moving her
wheelchair to the fridge. 'We usually have breakfast
and lunch in our cottage, and we go up to the
restaurant for dinner.'

There was a sound outside.

'Go and see what it is, Kirsty,' Laura suggested.

Kirsty went outside. There was a fence just beyond
the brick-paved *stoep* of the cottage, and on the other
side of the fence there were two hippopotamuses, busy
eating bales of grass that had just been thrown over
to them.

'My camera,' Kirsty said. 'Where's my camera? No
one at home will believe this!'

It was too late to go out game-viewing that day, but
after it was dark, sitting outside the thatched cottage,
Kirsty could hear the distant sounds of animals.

'Was that a lion?' she asked, awed.

'I think so,' Mark replied. 'And that was an
elephant, pretty far away.'

The stars were very clear in the black of the sky.
Clearer even than at Bloemenkloof, Kirsty thought.
Laura was right about this place, she thought; it really
is magic.

And there was even more magic the next morning,
when they rose while it was still dark—but dark and
warm, Kirsty thought wonderingly—to go on a bird

walk with the head ranger. Mark made tea while Kirsty got Laura up and to the bathroom, and then into her chair.

'Are you sure you'll be all right on your own?' she asked doubtfully.

'I'll be fine,' Laura assured her. 'Off you go—we'll have breakfast when you get back.'

Neither Kirsty nor Mark said anything as they walked over to the main complex, but as they reached there Mark told her that the game ranger would take small parties of guests on this dawn bird walk.

'Since this is a private game park,' he said, 'Jake never has many people here. And he always keeps the cottage we're in for friends.'

Kirsty knew that she would never forget that dawn walk in the bushveld. The grasslands were spangled with dew as the sun rose, and all around were the early morning sounds of the birds. They saw a fish eagle soaring high in the sky, and in a small wood they could hear the hooting of owls. The game ranger showed them the hole in a tree-trunk where a pearlspotted owl lived, and then, in the sky above them, there was a flash of blue.

'Look, Kirsty—a lilac-breasted roller,' Mark said urgently, his hand on her shoulder. 'See how he dives and rolls in the sky.'

His hand on her shoulder was warm, and there was no distance, no constraint in his voice as he showed her the beautiful little bird wheeling in the sky.

And then, realising, he removed his hand and turned away. And for Kirsty some of the wonder and magic was gone. Because it could all have been so different, she and Mark here together in this wonderful place. If only——

But it was too late for any if only, she reminded herself as she turned to where the game ranger was pointing out a glossy black bird with the unlikely name of Fork-tailed Drongo.

'Yes, it was wonderful,' she said in answer to Laura's

eager question, when they arrived back at the cottage.
Mark said that they had been fortunate to see a large
number of birds, and the new game ranger was
very good.

'I never mind how many birds we see; it's enough
just to be out walking over the bushveld at dawn,'
Laura said—and then she stopped, all too conscious,
Kirsty knew, of what she had just said. 'Walking over
the bushveld'.

But it took her only a moment to recover, and when
they had had breakfast it was Laura who suggested
that they go for a swim.

'There are only four of the cottages occupied, and
most folks will be out on the game drive, in the Land
Rover,' she said. 'So the pool should be quiet.'

They did have it to themselves, and Mark lifted
Laura into the water, and then sat on the edge, watch-
ing as Kirsty helped Laura to do the exercises Meg
Russell had shown her. When they had finished, and
Laura was back in her wheelchair, her towel wrapped
round her, Kirsty went back in for a quick swim.

She had bought a new one-piece costume in
Stellenbosch, because the bikini was obviously meant
just for sunbathing in. For a moment, now, she found
Mark's eyes resting on her, and she wondered if he
too was remembering that late-night swim, when she
had lost her bikini-top. And if he was remembering,
too, the kiss that had followed that.

No, Kirsty told herself determinedly, I will not waste
any more emotional energy on thinking about things
like that! What was it Gran always said? 'What's over
is over'.

The important thing, here and now, was to remember how much Laura had been counting on these few
days, and not to do or say anything that could spoil it
for her.

They walked back to the cottage, slowly, because of
the heat, their towels round them, and Mark pushing
Laura's chair.

'You're very good with Laura in the water,' Mark said a little awkwardly, joining her in the kitchen while Laura was out on the *stoep*. 'Meg Russell did say you've picked up very quickly what to do, and you've become very professional using the laser.'

'Thank you,' Kirsty replied, just as awkwardly. And then she said, with honesty, 'I'm very glad to be able to do something that's more professional in my care of Laura. And it isn't very difficult, you know.'

Unexpectedly, the doctor smiled.

'Perhaps not,' he agreed. 'But still, you do it well. Thank you, Kirsty.'

She thought that perhaps what he was really saying was, Thank you for staying on, for not walking out. And she thought, too, that perhaps Mark was also determined that they would not spoil this for Laura.

And so, a little later, when they had had lunch, and Kirsty said she wanted to walk up to the main complex for some postcards, she didn't react with an immediate refusal when Mark said he would go with her.

'Mad dogs and Englishmen,' Laura said. 'Too hot for me, at this time.'

'It's past midday, and even if you count me a mad dog you'd have to change the next bit to Scotswomen,' Mark pointed out. 'Put your hat on, Kirsty; Laura's right—it's mighty hot now.'

It wasn't far to the main complex, with the small restaurant, a gift shop and a reception area. Determinedly, she asked Mark more about Malalozi, and the animals they might see when they took a drive later in the afternoon.

'Towards sunset is a good time for game-viewing,' Mark said. He handed her a postcard. 'This one was taken from the air; it shows the extinct crater best.'

'I'll take that one,' Kirsty said. 'And these animal ones. That should be enough.'

It was as they were walking back together that Mark looked down at her and said, quite abruptly, 'Kirsty, there's something I want to say to you. I—I've been thinking about what you said, about Laura. I've actually talked to one or two people about it. Perhaps I was rather hasty. Perhaps it's worth considering.'

Kirsty didn't know what to say. After a moment, she asked him, carefully, what he was thinking of doing.

'I've talked to Bill Brown. He's going to arrange for Laura to see someone. Depending on that, he may suggest therapy.'

They had almost reached the cottage. Mark stopped. His eyes were very dark.

'What I'm really trying to say, Kirsty, is that I owe you an apology.' He held out his hand. 'I'm sorry,' he said simply.

There was nothing Kirsty could do but put her hand in his.

'I'm glad for Laura's sake,' she said carefully. 'I really do feel this could be the answer.'

But it doesn't change anything between the two of us, she found herself thinking as she sat down to write her postcards. In spite of what Mark said, I'm sure he still thinks that what I said was unforgivable. And I certainly think it was unforgivable of him to remind me in that way that I was in his employ. So—yes, I'm glad for Laura's sake, and that's all.

In the late afternoon, when the heat of the day had gone a little, they set off in the small Suzuki van for a game drive.

'The other cottage people have to go out of the camp and through the proper gate,' Mark said, taking the van slowly over the cattle grid, beside a notice that said 'No Admittance'. 'But Jake's personal guests are allowed to use this gate; it takes us directly into the reserve.'

They drove along a dirt road, dry and dusty. Kirsty, looking eagerly all around, saw a small herd of buck on a hillside. Impala, Mark and Laura said at the same time. And a little further on they saw, to Kirsty's delight, two white rhinos with three young ones. Then they drove on, towards a shimmer of water. There they drew up.

Immediately, the silence of the bushveld surrounded them.

'What now?' Kirsty asked, finding herself whispering.

'We wait,' Mark told her. 'The ranger says this is the best place just now; visitors have seen quite a lot of game here.'

Laura was the first to see the giraffes, half a dozen of them, making their slow and stately way towards the water, and then standing, their legs splayed, so that their long necks could reach down.

'Water buck coming now,' Mark said, pointing to the big, heavy beasts. A little later, a dozen or so zebras made their way down from the hillside, followed soon after that by some sable antelopes.

'I'm sorry the elephants didn't come,' Laura said regretfully as they headed back for the camp. 'Or any of the big cats—there are lions and leopards, and last year Jake got two cheetahs.'

'We'll come out early tomorrow morning,' Mark said, his big hands strong on the wheel as he turned on to the smaller dirt road that led back to the camp. 'I think morning is a better time.'

Just before they reached the private gate, he stopped. There, just a little way off the road, was a black rhino.

Kirsty, her camera in her hand, was about to scramble out.

'What do you think you're doing?' Mark said sternly.

'I'm just going to take a photo,' Kirsty protested. 'I won't go near him.'

Mark shook his head.

'Rule one in a game reserve—never, ever get out of your car,' he told her. 'You may not want to go near him, but he may come near you. And there could be a lion in that long grass there, just waiting for you!'

Kirsty, suitably sobered, took her photo through the window instead.

It was dusk when they got back to the cottage, the sudden African dusk that she always found surprising, with no real twilight between day and night. They were to have dinner in the restaurant that night, and Kirsty, changed into fresh jeans and and a sea-blue T-shirt, left Laura putting some make-up on, her wheelchair drawn up to the mirror.

'I'll just go outside,' Kirsty said. 'I love the quietness here when it's dark.'

Mark's bedroom door was closed as she went out. She walked past the other thatched cottages, only a few of them with lights on and other visitors there. From the hippo enclosure, she could hear the huge animals' grunts. Perhaps tomorrow they'll come near our house again, she thought as she turned back, approaching the cottage from the brick-paved *stoep* instead of through the door.

But before she was in sight of the *stoep* she stopped, hearing Mark's voice, raised.

'So you actually went to see him?' he asked. 'At his cottage?'

'Yes, I did,' Laura replied. 'And I'm going back again to see him. I don't want to do anything behind your back, Mark; that's why I'm telling you.'

For a moment there was silence, and then Laura's voice again, not quite steady.

'I'm sorry if you're angry, Mark. I've thought about this very carefully, and I intend going on seeing Jonathan. I—I'm twenty-three now, Mark; I'm old enough to make up my own mind.'

'I suppose you are,' Mark said after a moment. 'You're right, I have to accept that.' And then his voice hardened. 'What I find very hard to accept, though, is the deceit, yours and Kirsty's. Because, of course, Kirsty has to be in on this—if not actually suggesting it!'

The injustice of this was too much for Kirsty. She

walked round the corner of the house to the open door.

'And just what did you expect me to do?' she asked, hoping her voice was steady, hoping it didn't reflect the shaking she felt inside. 'Do you think I should have come telling tales to you?'

Mark strode across the room to her and his hand gripped her wrist, hard.

'What I expect is responsible behaviour from you,' he said tightly. 'Nothing more and nothing less!'

Kirsty lifted her chin.

'As you would from anyone you employed,' she returned, and she pulled her wrist away from him.

'Mark, I asked Kirsty to take me to the cottage,' Laura said shakily. 'She said was I sure, and I said yes. You can't blame her.'

'Can't I?' Mark asked scornfully. He looked at his watch. 'We're late,' he said tersely. 'I booked our table for seven-thirty.'

'I don't want to come,' Kirsty said.

Mark shrugged.

'Please yourself,' he said, and he turned Laura's chair to the door.

'I'll stay here with Kirsty,' Laura said, but Kirsty shook her head and said she'd rather be alone. Laura's blue eyes met hers, distressed, and Kirsty hoped that the younger girl saw that she really meant that.

When they had gone, Kirsty stood still in the middle of the room. How could he speak to me like that? she thought. How could he look at me the way he did? For a moment, she was close to tears, and then anger and resentment won, and How could he? became, How dare he?

Hardly knowing what she was doing, she snatched the keys of the Suzuki from the table where Mark had left them, wanting only to get right out of this house, this room. The van was parked outside, and she got into it and drove off with a screech of tyres that helped only a little towards relieving her feelings.

It was only when she had driven over the cattle grid

that she realised she was now in the game reserve.

And that, she thought, cooling down a little, was a silly thing to do, just because I was so angry. I'd better just find a turning-place and go right back.

There was a moon, but all at once it went behind a bank of clouds. Kirsty drove slowly, until she came to an intersection, with four other dirt roads going off at angles. She turned the van round, and headed back the way she had come. Or thought she had, until the moon, out from behind the clouds, showed her an unfamiliar copse of trees where the gate should have been.

She drove on, determined not to give way to her rising panic. So many roads—which one was the right one?

Suddenly, there was a sputter from the engine, and then it died down. As it did, Kirsty remembered Mark saying when they'd got back earlier that he'd have to get petrol. She peered at the gauge. Yes, it was empty.

The silence of the game reserve was all around her, now that there was no sound from the car.

Mark had said never to get out of your car in a game reserve. Not that she was tempted to, she thought.

I'll just have to sit here and wait, she told herself. Until—until—until what? Mark and Laura might not realise for some time that she had taken the van. And, she realised painfully, even if they did they would think that she would have more sense than to come into the game reserve on her own, at night.

So she was alone here, in the silence and the stillness of the African night.

Then, somewhere, she heard the roar of a lion.

I'm not alone, Kirsty thought, her heart thudding unsteadily. There are all these animals. And that one sounded an awful lot closer than I want it to be!

CHAPTER THIRTEEN

DON'T panic, Kirsty told herself.

But it wasn't easy to keep calm, to think rationally, alone here in the middle of the game reserve, with that not too distant roar.

And was that a rustle, a branch of a tree breaking, somewhere even nearer?

The worst that can happen, Kirsty decided, was that she would have to stay here until morning.

The moon was behind clouds again, and she peered out, And realised that that wasn't the worst thing—the worst thing would be to look out, like this, and see some large and fierce animal peering in at her. All right, she should be safe, as long as she was in the car, with the windows tightly closed, but it wouldn't be very pleasant. And hadn't there been a newspaper report about some rogue elephant who had taken a dislike to a car and trampled on it?

She switched on the lights. It would run the battery flat, but, since there was no petrol and the car couldn't move anyway, that didn't really matter. Someone just might see the lights and, even if they didn't surely the lights would keep animals away?

Some time afterwards—it felt like a long time, but she wasn't sure—she wondered why it was possible to feel shivery when the night was so warm. You're just frightened, she told herself scornfully, but identifying the reason didn't really help, and she sat behind the wheel of the little van, her arms hugged around herself.

Was that a light, coming towards her?

Cautiously, she opened the window a sliver, and—yes, she could hear the sound of a car, and surely it was getting closer; the lights were definitely coming this way.

A large car drew up right beside her, with a protesting squeal of brakes.

'Open your door and move along,' Mark Barnard said tersely.

Kirsty unlocked the driver's door and moved along. In one movement, it seemed, Mark was out of the big car and in beside her, the door slammed behind him.

It didn't need the gleam of moonlight to show her how angry he was. Angry? Angry, she realised, wasn't a strong enough word.

'What the hell do you think you're doing?' he asked furiously.

And now that he was here, now that she wasn't alone, it was suddenly all too much for Kirsty. She burst into tears and flung herself into his arms, as well as she could, in the confines of the small van.

There was a moment of resistance, his arms and his body unyielding, and then his arms were holding her close and he was patting her shoulder and murmuring something—it didn't matter what—into her hair.

'How did you—find me?' she managed to ask at last, unevenly.

'One of the rangers saw your lights suddenly come on.' He took out his handkerchief and dried her tears, his big hands, so skilful in his work, suddenly awkward. 'Until then it never dawned on me that you might have come into the reserve. I thought you'd just driven off somewhere around the camp.' He shook her, but quite gently. 'That was a stupid thing to do, Kirsty.'

'I didn't mean to come in here,' Kirsty admitted, her voice still unsteady. 'And I'd forgotten that there wasn't much petrol. And—and I took the wrong turning, and the petrol ran out, and Mark, I'm sure I heard a lion.'

'You probably did,' Mark agreed equably.

In the moonlight, he looked down at her.

'You're not going to start crying again, are you?' he asked, and the gentleness and the warmth of his voice unnerved her so much that she almost did. 'I haven't got another handkerchief.'

And then, almost without pausing, he said, 'Kirsty, I'm sorry for the things I said, for the way I spoke to you. I had no right to, and there's no justification for any of it.'

'You were worried about Laura,' Kirsty reminded him. 'People do funny things when they're worried. And I'm always talking back to you, and that makes you angry.'

'You do have a knack of getting under my skin,' Mark agreed.

Unbelievably, there was warm laughter in his voice. And in the moonlight she could see that he was smiling.

Kirsty realised then that his arms were still around her, holding her close to him.

'I'm all right now,' she said, wriggling a little. 'I was just—just a wee bit nervous, until you got here.'

'And here I was thinking you were just so delighted to see me,' he said, and his arms held her more firmly.

'Well, maybe I was,' Kirsty admitted after a moment.

And then, just before the clouds hid the moon again, she saw that he was no longer smiling.

'Kirsty,' he said unsteadily. 'Oh, Kirsty.'

In the darkness his lips found hers, searching, demanding. A demand that her whole body responded to as she clung to him, as she returned his passion.

Suddenly, he let her go.

'This darned van is cramping my style,' he said, not quite steadily.

He opened the door.

'What are you doing?' Kirsty asked, alarmed. 'We mustn't get out of the car.'

'Only to get into the other one,' he assured her. 'It's only two steps. Look, you move over behind the wheel as I get out—that's right.'

In one movement, then, he lifted her out of the van and into the car.

But into the back seat.

'Unfinished business,' he murmured as he closed the door.

He took her in his arms again. And Kirsty, remembering afterwards, could never be sure which of them moved closer first, whether Mark began to kiss her or whether she kissed him. All she knew was that the interruption had done nothing to change what both of them knew was going to happen.

Later—much later—she stirred in his arms.

'It's a long time,' she murmured, 'since I was kissed in the back seat of a car.'

'Kissed?' Mark said, his lips against her hair. 'And I thought you were a girl who liked to be honest—to call a spade a spade.'

In the darkness Kirsty could feel her cheeks grow warm.

'All right,' she agreed, 'a wee bit more than kissing. I'd better get myself tidy before we go back.'

She sat up straight.

'What about Laura?' she asked, alarmed and ashamed of herself that this was the first time she had thought of her patient.

'I left her with the chief ranger's wife,' Mark told her. 'We'll go back there now. And tomorrow I'll come with the ranger and collect the van.'

As they drove back towards the camp, Kirsty said, 'Are they not going to wonder why we've been such an awful long time?'

'An awful long time? I wouldn't call it awful,' Mark said.

'That's just a Scottish way of saying it,' Kirsty replied, with dignity. And then, realising that he was teasing her, and that she liked it, she said, 'Oh, Mark, you know what I mean.'

His hand covered hers for a moment, before he negotiated the cattle grid into the camp.

'Yes, I know what you mean, and actually we haven't been that long, *meisie*.'

'What did you call me?' Kirsty asked him.

'*Meisie*,' he said, a little embarrassed. 'It's an Afrikaans word—our mother was Afrikaans, so we grew up speaking both languages. It just means girl—you'd probably say lass in Scotland.'

He switched off the engine as they drew up outside the ranger's cottage.

'I think you could say it's a term of endearment,' he said softly.

'A term of endearment. I—like that,' Kirsty told him.

His lips brushed hers, just for a moment.

'That's certainly how I meant it,' he said.

Surprisingly, Kirsty thought later, there weren't many questions, either from Laura or from the ranger and his wife. Mark explained that Kirsty hadn't realised she was driving into the game reserve, and had then run out of petrol. Though how anyone could drive over a cattle grid without knowing it was hard to believe, Kirsty knew.

Laura looked white and anxious when they went in, and Kirsty was very conscious of her eyes going from her brother to Kirsty herself, questioning, concerned. But then she gradually relaxed.

'Tea and sandwiches,' the ranger's wife said briskly. 'I'm sure we could all do with something.'

'I certainly could,' Kirsty admitted, realising now that she was ravenous.

'You did well on the sandwiches, Kirsty,' Laura said later as Mark pushed her wheelchair back to their cottage.

'I didn't have any dinner,' Kirsty defended herself. 'Anyway, Mark didn't do too badly either, as someone who had!'

'Oh, well,' Mark said easily, 'a little bit of excitement and activity always gives me an appetite.'

In the light above their cottage door he looked at Kirsty, and she knew very well that he had seen the warm tide of colour in her cheeks.

Laura asked no questions when they were alone in their room, and Kirsty was grateful for that, grateful to be able to lie awake, in the warm darkness of the summer night, remembering how it had felt to be in Mark's arms and knowing that he was so close to her, under the same roof. But close in more than physical distance now.

There wasn't much chance for them to be alone the next day, for they had arranged to go out in the Land Rover with the ranger, for a game drive, early in the morning, and later that day there was a film for all the guests, showing how the game park had been started, the operations to bring in the animals, the building of the cottages, the ongoing commitment to conservation.

But in the evening Laura, her eyes wide and innocent, said that she wanted some of the wildlife notepaper from the gift shop, and would Mark and Kirsty mind walking up to get it for her?

'And don't hurry back,' she said, 'I'm almost finished your P.D.James, Mark, and I can't bear to leave it.'

'Do you think Laura knows?' Mark said as they walked up to the main building. He took her hand in his and swung it lightly as they walked.

'Knows what?' Kirsty asked, her own eyes as wide and as innocent as Laura's had been.

He stopped, under the eaves of one of the empty cottages.

'That we need some time alone,' he murmured as his lips found hers.

'We can't do this,' Kirsty said faintly.

'Do what?' Mark asked, and kissed her again.

Later—much later, Kirsty thought hazily—she managed to continue what she had been about to say.

'This,' she said. 'This falling into each other's arms the moment we're alone.'

'Why not?' Mark asked reasonably. 'We're making up for lost time, and do we have a lot of lost time to make up for! An awful lot of lost time,' he said, with a fair attempt at a Scottish accent.

When they had bought Laura's notepaper, they sat down at one of the little tables overlooking the wide sweep of grassland that the camp encircled. There were no clouds, and the full moon shimmered on the water-hole nearest to the camp.

'It's magic,' Kirsty said softly.

'It is,' Mark agreed. He put his hand over hers. 'Kirsty, there are a few things we have to talk about, you and I. One of them is Simon.'

'Simon?' Kirsty repeated, taken aback.

'You seem to get on so well, you and Simon,' Mark said slowly. 'You laugh together, you seem to have fun when you go out. He's closer to your own age than I am, and he's been a heck of a lot nicer to you!'

There was no one around, and even if there had been Kirsty wouldn't have cared. She leaned closer to Mark and kissed him, slowly, warmly.

'Do you really think, after last night,' she said, not quite steadily, 'that you should even be asking me about Simon? You must know, Mark, that there is only you, and there always has been only you, but I wouldn't admit it to myself.'

'Because I was so horrible to you?' he asked.

'I wasn't particularly pleasant to you,' Kirsty replied. 'Yes, that, but most of all because you weren't free.'

'Ah, yes—Helen,' Mark said after a moment. 'I suppose we'd better talk about Helen.'

'Only if you want to,' Kirsty said, meaning it.

He took her hand, touching each finger in turn, gently, and then turning her hand over so that he could kiss the palm.

'There isn't really much to say,' he said after a while. 'We've known each other for years, we've gone around in the same crowd—getting engaged seemed a logical step. Look, we were having problems before you came on the scene, because of my work, but——'

'But?' Kirsty prompted him.

In the moonlight she could see the slow, warm smile as he looked down at her.

'But in spite of what I thought about you—that you were the most exasperating, interfering girl I had ever met—there was this incredible thing between us, different from anything Helen and I had even come close to. I was fighting that, Kirsty. And not too successfully. And realising that—there wasn't anything of substance between Helen and me.'

'I was fighting it too,' Kirsty admitted. 'I kept telling myself it was just a physical attraction, nothing more.'

She stopped then, because it hadn't actually been said between them, not in so many words.

And the incredible thing, the wonderful thing, she realised later, was that Mark understood right away.

'But it's that, and more, isn't it?' he said, his voice low. 'So much more.'

'We were talking about Helen,' Kirsty reminded him after a moment.

'Oh, yes, so we were,' Mark agreed. He shrugged. 'Well, we talked, Helen and I, and we agreed that my work would always be a problem for her. She wasn't heartbroken by any means. It made sense to her that we should call it a day. I hear she's seeing a lawyer now—his hours are bound to be better than a GP's.'

It was as they were walking back to the cottage that Kirsty asked him what he thought of doing about Laura.

'I don't know yet,' Mark admitted.

He looked down at her.

'That was a tough one,' he said, 'when you made me see the pressure I had been putting on her. I find it hard to forgive myself for that.' His hand tightened on hers. 'I was mad about what you said, but when I cooled down I had to admit that there just might be some truth in it. And some faint possibility that you could be right about Laura's paralysis. I talked to a couple of people, and it began to seem more than just a faint possibility. And then, just after I'd swallowed my pride and admitted that to you, Laura decided to stand up for herself and tell me that she intended going on seeing her artist.'

He glanced down at her.

'Then I got mad again, and blamed you, and that was unforgivable. Laura pointed that out to me well and truly, after we left you.'

At the door of the cottage, he put his arms around her and held her close to him.

'The rest you know,' he said softly.

'The rest I know,' Kirsty agreed.

Laura looked up from her book when they went in.

'Good timing,' she said. 'I've just finished; I was checking the beginning again, making sure I'd tied up all the loose ends. Every bit as good as you said, Mark.'

And then, looking from one to the other, she remarked, 'Glad to see you two are friends again. You are, aren't you?'

Mark looked at Kirsty, one eyebrow raised.

'Yes, I suppose you could say that,' he agreed gravely. 'Would you agree, Kirsty?'

'Yes, I think so,' Kirsty said quickly. 'What time do we leave tomorrow? Do I have to pack tonight?'

Mark shook his head and said there would be time in the morning. And then, looking down at Laura, he said quietly, 'We haven't had time to talk, Laura, since yesterday. I've said to Kirsty that I'm sorry for the way I reacted, and I'm saying it now to you. You are right, of course; you are old enough to make your own decisions. I've been very stubborn about that. I would like to meet your Jonathan again, on a different basis this time.'

Laura's blue eyes were on his face, as if, Kirsty thought with compassion, she had to be certain that her brother really meant this.

'I would like that too, Mark,' she said at last, and her voice was steady. 'Thank you.'

* * *

When they left Malalozi, the pilot flying low to let them have a last glimpse of the vast sweep of the game reserve, set in the heart of the extinct volcano, the cluster of cottages at one end, and the open plains at the other, it seemed to Kirsty that they had been there much longer than a few days.

But so much had happened, so much had changed, no wonder it seemed longer, she thought. It would always be a very special place for her.

'We'll come back again,' Mark murmured, his head close to hers, as the plane swung round and headed south.

Simon was waiting at the airport to meet them, and he and Mark talked about the weather, about the grape harvest, as they headed for Bloemenkloof. It hadn't bothered Mark, Kirsty knew, that Simon had swung her off her feet with an exuberant kiss when he'd met them. For a moment, when Simon had set her down, Mark's eyes had met hers, and she had known it was all right.

There were calls for Mark, when they reached the house, calls he had to return, even a hospital visit he had to make. Laura was tired after the journey, faint shadows under her blue eyes, and Kirsty, with Sarah's support, told her firmly that she was to have an early night.

On her own, with Mark still out, Kirsty finished the letters she had stared to write in the game reserve, listening for the sound of Mark's car returning. Eventually, she gave up, had a bath, and got ready for bed. She was brushing her hair, when she heard a soft knock at her door. Pulling on her short blue cotton dressing-gown, she hurried to open it.

'I just wanted to say goodnight,' Mark said, looking down at her, and then, carefully, 'What I said about Helen before—I still have to give her time, Kirsty, let her make it clear to the world in general that she's all right.'

Kirsty stood on tiptoe and kissed him.

'Don't worry, Mark,' she assured him. 'I know that, and we can wait.' She added, 'I'm glad you came to say goodnight.'

He held her close to him, his lips warm and urgent on hers. And then, quite abruptly, he let her go.

'Get inside and lock your door, *meisie*,' he told her. 'Otherwise I don't think I can answer for myself.'

And I don't think I could answer for myself either, Kirsty thought, smiling, as she closed her door—without feeling the need to lock it.

The next day Laura phoned Jonathan and asked him to come that evening.

'He says he'd rather not come for dinner,' she told Kirsty. She smiled, but her blue eyes were concerned. 'He'll come along later. I think he's considerably more nervous than he would admit to. He and Mark did meet before, but—well, you know how Mark can be, and that made Jonathan very defensive, and—probably a bit aggressive.'

It was during dinner that Mark told Laura she was to see the orthopaedic surgeon, Bill Brown, the next day.

'Is there any real point in that?' Laura asked. Her voice was steady, but Kirsty saw that her hands were clasped together, very tightly. 'Nothing has changed, after all.'

'No, that's true,' Mark agreed. For a moment his eyes met Kirsty's. 'But Bill did say he'd like to see you again after you'd had some phsyiotherapy. And he's suggesting that you meet a colleague of his, Andrew Morton.'

'Is he an orthopaedic surgeon too?' Laura asked.

Mark hesitated.

'Well, no,' he said after a moment. 'He's a psy-chiatrist. Bill thought that talking to him might help you to come to terms with things.'

He had told Kirsty briefly, when he got home, that Dr Brown had suggested this approach, had said that it would not be a good idea for Mark himself to let

Laura know of the possibility of her paralysis being psychosomatic.

'That's probably a good idea,' Laura agreed steadily. She looked at the big grandfather clock. 'I'd like to tidy myself a bit before Jonathan comes. No, stay where you are, Kirsty; I can manage.'

'Expertly, now, she wheeled her chair out of the room and along the passage.

'I think I'll just see that she's all right,' Kirsty said after a moment.

'Yes, do,' Mark said.

Kirsty went along the corridor. The door to Laura's room was open, and she went in.

Laura had stopped in the middle of the room, and she was sitting in her wheelchair, crying silently, her face hidden in her hands.

How could we have been so selfish? Kirsty thought, her heart aching for Laura. How can we even begin to think of our own happiness while Laura is in that wheelchair and unable to walk?

CHAPTER FOURTEEN

THERE will be time for us, for Mark and me, Kirsty thought as she stood beside the weeping girl. For now, it's Laura we have to think about, Laura we have to put before anything else.

'Laura,' she said gently, and she put her hand on the younger girl's shoulder. 'Jonathan will be here soon. Are you going to be all right?'

Laura lifted her face from her hands.

'Yes, I'll be all right,' she said, not quite steadily. 'I'll give my face a splash and put some eyeshadow on.'

She pushed her wheelchair through to the bathroom, and when she had done that she looked up and smiled.

'Will I do?' she asked.

'You'll do,' Kirsty told her, and she bent and hugged her.

Halfway along the wide hall Laura's hand on the brake stopped the wheelchair.

'You know,' she said slowly, 'if I had to accept this I could and I would. If I'd been told that some vital nerve had been severed, I think I could handle that. It would be easier for me to accept, if someone could give me a clear-cut reason. Does that sound foolish, Kirsty?'

'No, it doesn't,' Kirsty said with truth. 'I feel a wee bit like that myself sometimes.' She hesitated and then said, carefully, that perhaps they would all find the visit to the orthopaedic surgeon and the psychiatrist helpful.

Laura shrugged.

'Perhaps,' she agreed, without any real conviction. She released the brake. 'Sounds as if Jonathan is here already; we'd better rescue him from Mark. Or Mark from him, maybe.'

'Whatever,' Kirsty said, more than a little apprehensively.

Both men looked round with considerable relief when Kirsty and Laura went in.

'Ah, there you are,' Mark said. 'I was just asking Jonathan if he'd like a drink. How about you two? A glass of wine? You like our own Riesling, don't you, Kirsty? Jonathan—white as well, or would you prefer red?'

'I'll have a glass of your Shiraz, thanks,' Jonathan said.

And I'm sure, Kirsty thought ruefully, he wasn't meaning to sound a bit abrupt; it's just his way of covering up being nervous.

'I have a bottle of the 1982 open,' Mark said, handing Jonathan a glass.

'A good year, that one,' Jonathan replied. 'But surely the 1983 is even better?'

And I don't know which of them won that point, Kirsty thought, her eyes meeting Laura's for a moment.

That was the pattern, she thought later, for most of the evening. Both men were fairly polite, but just a little aggressive. They discussed the wine harvest, they discussed the exhibition of Jonathan's work held recently in Stellenbosch, and—with considerable relief, Kirsty thought—they all talked about the Malalozi trip.

Just after Jonathan said that he thought he should be going, Laura said unexpectedly, 'Wait a minute. I want to show you something, Mark. Kirsty, would you mind bringing my picture from the desk?'

Kirsty brought through the picture Jonathan had given Laura for Christmas, and handed it to Laura, leaving it to her to turn it round so that Mark could see it.

Remembering her own reaction when she'd first seen Jonathan's work, Kirsty wasn't surprised to see Mark's. He looked at the painting for a long time, then he stood up and walked further back, still studying it.

'I like that,' he said. 'I really do.' Then he added, turning to Jonathan, 'I'm sorry, that sounded as if I didn't expect to like it.'

'But you didn't,' Jonathan said, and he smiled. 'You thought it was going to be cubist, or abstract, or so modern that you wouldn't have the slightest idea what it was supposed to be!'

And it was the first time, in the whole evening, Kirsty thought with relief, that either of them sounded real and natural!

'I suppose I did,' Mark agreed. He hesitated, but only for a moment. 'I'd like to see some more of your work, Jonathan. Is that exhibition still on?'

Jonathan said that no, it was over, but the gallery had anything that hadn't been sold.

Then Kirsty suggested a cup of coffee before Jonathan went, and she went through to the kitchen to make it.

'Bring some of Sarah's melktert, please, Kirsty,' Laura said, from the door.

Her cheeks were flushed, and her eyes bright, Kirsty was delighted to see. She was sure Mark would have seen, too.

'Didn't you think Laura looked the better for that?' she said to him a little later, when Laura had gone to the front door to say goodbye to Jonathan, and Kirsty was putting the coffee-cups and the wine glasses on the tray.

'Yes, she did,' Mark agreed.

He took the tray from her and set it down. Then he took her in his arms.

'Laura will be back any minute,' Kirsty protested.

'I doubt it,' Mark said. 'Anyway, I'd be surprised if she hasn't guessed.'

He kissed her, his lips gentle on hers, warm and gentle, and then not at all gentle.

'I've been waiting all night to do that,' he said, his voice low. 'To see you sitting across the room from

me, smiling, and that way you have of pushing your
hair back from your face—stop wriggling, *meisie*, and
come here.'

Somehow, rather to Kirsty's surprise, they were
sitting on the couch now.

'Better than the back seat of the car, don't you
think?' Mark murmured. And then he said, delighted,
'You're blushing, Kirsty; I love that. How did I do
with Jonathan tonight?'

'Och, the two of you were like two dogs wondering
if you were to fight or not,' Kirsty told him. 'Both of
you with your hackles up. But thanks to Laura thinking
of the painting, I think you ended up not too bad!'

Laura came back then, and Kirsty, having just been
well and truly kissed herself, thought that it was more
than likely that there had been at the very least a
goodnight kiss between Laura and Jonathan.

And later, when Laura was in bed, and Kirsty had
made sure she was comfortable, and had everything
she needed, the younger girl called her back as she
was leaving the room.

'Kirsty', she said a little hesitantly, 'I'm not being
nosy, but—well, I can't help seeing that things have
changed between you and Mark. I've seen the way
you look at each other. I know that Mark will feel he
has to give Helen time, but I just wanted you to
know—I think it's great!'

Kirsty, with one hand on the doorknob, looked at
this girl she had come to know so well. There was no
doubt that Laura meant every word.

'Thanks, Laura,' she said. 'Thanks for saying that.'

It wasn't only Laura who had guessed how things
were between Mark and her, she began to realise.
Sometimes she found Sarah's eyes resting on her
thoughtfully and then moving to Mark. Kirsty hoped
that it was a small nod of approval she saw. And then
there was Simon. He hadn't said anything, since they'd
got back from Malalozi, but when he'd asked her if
she would like to come with him to a party, and she'd

said, Thank you, but no, he'd said he understood. And
Kirsty had a strong feeling that he did, completely.

The next day she took Laura through to the private
hospital just outside Cape Town, where they had gone
before, to see the orthopaedic surgeon. Mark had
hoped to go as well, but one of his patients had to
have an emergency removal of part of the stomach,
after a recurring duodenal ulcer, and he was assisting
the surgeon. Kirsty waited while Mark's friend Bill
Brown saw Laura, and after half an hour the specialist
came out to the waiting-room.

'Nurse Cameron, isn't it?' he said. 'I've just rung
through to Dr Morton; he'll see Laura now—along
the corridor, Room 301.'

Kirsty could see how tense Laura was as she turned
the wheelchair into the psychiatrist's rooms. And actually, she thought, I feel pretty tense myself, just
waiting!

But Laura looked considerably less tense when Dr
Morton opened his door about forty minutes later, and
handed over the wheelchair to Kirsty.

'How was it?' Kirsty asked cautiously as they headed
away from Cape Town.

'I don't know what I expected,' Laura said after a
moment, 'but really we just talked. He's an easy man
to talk to.'

'What did you talk about?' Kirsty asked.

'Oh, all sorts of things,' Laura said. And then,
slowly, 'I suppose he's trying to find out what sort of
person I am, so that he can help me to—to come to
terms with this. He said he'd like me to see him again.'

'How do you feel about that?' Kirsty asked.

Laura was silent for a little while.

'I don't mind,' she said at last. 'Perhaps it is helpful,
talking to someone who isn't too closely involved in
the whole thing.'

She smiled, but Kirsty could see the effort it took.

'Meanwhile we stick with the physiotherapy, with
the daily exercises, and the swimming, Dr Brown says.'

Kirsty was longing to hear what the psychiatrist thought, after seeing Laura and talking to her. But she had to wait until the following evening, after Laura was in bed.

'Have you heard from Dr Morton?' she asked Mark as soon as they were alone.

Mark nodded.

'He phoned this afternoon. He would like to see me, he says, rather than discuss it on the phone. I can manage tomorrow afternoon, but I really want you there too. How could we work that, without taking Laura?'

'Well,' Kirsty said slowly, 'Laura did suggest a while back that there were places in Cape Town you should show me. Perhaps if you were to suggest us doing that?'

It was, in fact, no problem at all. When the subject was broached the next morning, Laura seemed to be delighted by the prospect of Mark and Kirsty going to Cape Town on their own.

'And perhaps I'll ring Jonathan and ask him to come here and visit me,' she suggested guilelessly.

'Yes, that's an idea,' Mark agreed after a moment.

'I couldn't very well say no,' he said to Kirsty, that afternoon, as he drew into a parking bay at the hospital. 'Could I?'

'Did you want to?' Kirsty asked him.

He thought about that, then, 'No, I didn't,' he said. 'No, I think I made up my mind too quickly about him.'

He looked down at her as they walked into the foyer.

'Thanks for that, Kirsty,' he said quietly. 'For giving me a second chance on that.'

Dr Morton nodded when Mark said that he wanted Kirsty to be with him to hear about the psychiatrist's meeting with Laura.

'Yes, Laura spoke a great deal about you, Nurse Cameron,' he said. 'And I gather from Bill Brown that you were the first to consider the possibility of hysterical paralysis—a conversion reaction.'

It will probably take him quite a while to get to the point, Mark thought, but he was wrong.

'I think you're right about that,' Dr Morton said then. 'Laura has eliminated her anxiety by producing physical symptoms that protect her from dealing with it. Often the conflict and the cause are much more obscure than with Laura.'

He looked from Kirsty to Mark, and then back to Kirsty again.

'I gather you worked that out for yourself, Nurse, Laura's conflict between what her brother expected of her, what her young man expected, and what she could handle.'

'Mark. . .' Kirsty murmured, and he could see that she was uncertain of how he would take this.

'It's all right,' he said to her evenly. 'I told Bill Brown exactly what you said, and he passed it on.' He looked at the psychiatrist. 'How do we handle it?' he asked, knowing he sounded more abrupt than he meant to. 'How do we get Laura to realise that she can walk? I'm sure it isn't as simple as just telling her that she can.'

'No, I'm afraid not,' Dr Morton said. He hesitated. 'There are two ways I would suggest. One is counselling—therapy—we let Laura work it out for herself. That can take a long time, and in a case like this the longer Laura believes she can't walk, the more difficult it becomes.'

Mark leaned forward.

'And your other suggestion?' he asked.

'I have had some success with hypnotherapy in treating psychosomatic illnesses,' Dr Morton said.

'Hypnotherapy?' Mark repeated. 'You mean hypnotise Laura, and tell her she can walk?'

He saw Kirsty glance at him anxiously, and he knew that he hadn't been able to hide his suspicion and his disbelief.

'Not quite, Dr Barnard,' the psychiatrist said, without taking offence. 'Actually, most GPs have this reaction. No, what I'm talking about is a light trance—so light, Laura won't even know—and I will make a suggestion that perhaps she will be able to take in, in that state, about the possibility of walking. Look, I have to say that there is no guarantee about this. Neurosis is an unconscious attempt at self-defence. What we need is for Laura to see, on a conscious level, that she doesn't need this self-defence any longer.'

His grey eyes were steady.

'That, Dr Barnard, is up to you,' he went on. 'You have to let Laura see that you are prepared to let her live her own life, to make her own decisions. Even to make her own mistakes.'

'I hope I've begun to do that,' Mark said.

There was a small, agitated movement from Kirsty.

'I'm sure you have,' she said, obviously unable to keep silent any longer. She looked at the psychiatrist. 'Really, Dr Morton, Laura can see the change—she's already beginning to make her own decisions.'

'Then shall we try?' Dr Morton said. 'As I said, I can't guarantee anything, but it's well worth trying, to short-circuit extensive therapy.' He walked to the door with them, and left them to make another appointment for Laura. 'As soon as possible,' he told his reception-ist firmly.

Outside the small hospital they stopped, and Kirsty put her hand on Mark's arm. He covered it with his own, more glad than ever that she was there with him.

'I don't know what I expected,' he said slowly, 'but it certainly wasn't trying something like that. But—well, Bill Brown thinks highly of this fellow, and so do a few folks I've spoken to.'

'It's worth trying,' Kirsty said firmly, and then, 'What are we going to tell Laura we did with our afternoon in Cape Town?'

Mark opened the car door for her.

'I'm afraid it will be rather a whistle-stop tour,' he said regretfully. 'Tell you what, we'll have tea at

Rhodes Memorial, then we'll drive up Signal Hill.'

They had tea and scones with cream, in the little restaurant above the memorial to Cecil Rhodes, with its eight stone lions, and its equestrian bronze statue, at the foot of the huge flight of stone steps.

As they were leaving, they looked down at Cape Town, spread out below them, and Mark showed Kirsty the distant blue mountains behind Bloemenkloof. He told her that she would find the view from Signal Hill even more spectacular, because it was higher, and she agreed.

'But I'll bring you here at night; it's wonderful to see the lights of Cape Town spread out below you. We don't have time to drive down to the waterfront,' he said regretfully. 'We'll save that for another time.'

She seemed to know that he didn't want to talk any more about Laura right now, and on the way back to Stellenbosch she asked him about his patients.

'I've never seen an angiogram done,' she said regretfully, when he told her about Mrs Wingate. 'Not that I've ever wanted to do theatre work, really—I prefer closer contact with patients—but it does sound fascinating.'

'I feel the same about surgery,' Mark agreed. 'It is interesting, and sometimes when I'm assisting I think maybe—— But then I go back to my patients, and I know I prefer being a GP.'

'And what about Mrs Wingate?' Kirsty asked. 'What did the angiogram show?'

An obstruction to the artery, he told her, too big to be dealt with by angioplasty; it would have to be a bypass. He then told her about Ken Harris, and his multiple sclerosis, and how he was back at home, once again in remission.

'The week in hospital helped,' he said, thinking about Ken. 'The treatment with ACTH made a difference, and so did the daily oil baths. But the most helpful thing was that Greta, his wife, realised that she doesn't have to cope alone—she can handle whatever happens next all the better because she's had the break.'

He glanced at her.

'Sorry, Kirsty,' he said, 'I get a bit carried away. Stop me when you've had enough.'

Her cheeks were pink with indignation.

'Don't even think that,' she told him. 'I love hearing about your patients!'

He could see that she meant it.

For a moment, he took his hand from the wheel, and covered one of her small brown hands with his.

And I always will want to hear about your patients, Kirsty thought. But she didn't say it—for even to think of the word 'always' made her breath stop in her throat.

Jonathan had just left when they got back to Bloemenkloof, Laura told them.

'You should have asked him to stay and have supper with us,' Mark said.

'Do you mean that?' Laura asked, her blue eyes on his face.

Mark didn't hesitate. 'Yes, I do,' he said steadily. 'It's time he and I got to know each other.'

Laura took a deep breath.

'Then next time he comes, I'll do that,' she said. She looked at Kirsty. 'Now tell me what you did in Cape Town.'

Kirsty told her about having tea at Rhodes Memorial, and about driving up Signal Hill.

'You mean that's all you did?' Laura asked, wide-eyed, but fortunately didn't ask for any more details.

Just as Kirsty managed not to ask for details when Laura had her next session with the psychiatrist.

She didn't actually know how she'd expected Laura to look, she thought afterwards, but there was nothing different about the fair-haired girl in the wheelchair as Kirsty took her out to the car. Maybe a wee bit sleepy—or just drowsy? she wondered. And decided that she was seeing what she thought she should see.

It would seem funny, though, she thought, if she didn't say anything at all.

'He's a very soothing sort of person,' Laura said suddenly, just as Kirsty was wondering how she could ask how the session had gone. 'I can't remember what we talked about, really, but I feel kind of rested.' She smiled. 'I suppose I was surprised that he doesn't have a couch, but that big armchair makes you feel very relaxed.'

It was foolish, Kirsty told herself over the next few days, to be watching Laura, wondering if anything would happen, wondering how anything would happen, if it did.

After a week, Mark told her that he was going to talk to Jonathan.

'He has a right to know,' he said quietly. 'He has as much right as you and I do, Kirsty. Perhaps more. It's a clear night—I'll walk up to the cottage.'

It was late when he came back, but Kirsty had felt that she had to wait up.

'How did he take it?' she asked Mark as they sat down on the swing seat on the *stoep*.

'Better than I did,' Mark said slowly, 'considering that although I was admitting that I was part of the problem I was telling him that so was he.'

In the moonlight he looked down at her.

'Jonathan has an idea,' he said then. 'I'll have to check it out with Dr Morton, but—well, Jonathan thinks that he and I should pretend to quarrel, pretend Jonathan is walking out. Perhaps the shock of that, combined with the suggestion made to Laura in the light trance, could make a breakthrough.'

'What if it doesn't work?' Kirsty asked doubtfully. 'What if Laura just sits there, and Jonathan walks out? Surely that would make things worse for her?'

'I wondered about that,' Mark admitted. 'But we thought I would back down quickly, and we'd make up the quarrel.'

Kirsty shook her head.

'I don't know,' she said. 'It all seems a wee bit risky to me.'

Privately, she thought that the psychiatrist would never give his approval to this. But the next night Mark told her that Dr Morton had said that in principle he thought it was worth trying, although they shouldn't in any circumstances expect that Laura would get out of her chair and walk. Nothing as dramatic as that. He did agree, though, that it could be a breakthrough, it could be a beginning.

'But he says don't be disappointed if it doesn't work,' Mark said. 'And also to back down on the quarrel quickly, in that case.'

The next morning, before Mark left for work, he suggested to Laura that she might ask Jonathan to have supper with them. Laura's face lit up, and all Kirsty's misgivings returned in full force. Maybe we shouldn't be trying this, she thought worriedly. But Dr Morton had said that the longer Laura's paralysis went on, the more difficult it could be to deal with. So. . .

But I hope they can carry it off, she thought more than once that evening, sensing the tension between the two men throughout the meal.

Laura, she could see, was all too conscious of it too. And because of that, perhaps, Kirsty thought, the quarrel, when it came, was more convincing to her.

Because one thing's for sure, she found herself thinking—Mark is a better doctor than he is an actor.

Jonathan seemed to manage better, and the way he took offence when Mark asked him how many pictures he had sold at the last exhibition was very convincing.

'I suppose you're back on the penniless artist line,' he said belligerently.

Mark stood up.

'I just want to know that you will be able to support my sister,' he said.

'And I don't think it's any of your business!' Jonathan retorted.

'Mark, Jonathan, please don't,' Laura said, looking from one to the other. 'Can't we just——?'

Now Jonathan stood up.

'I'm not staying here to be insulted,' he said.

'All right, then, go,' Mark flung at him. 'And don't bother coming back!'

Jonathan strode to the door.

Kirsty could feel her heart thudding unsteadily.

'No!' Laura said. 'Don't go, Jonathan!'

Her hands were on the sides of her wheelchair. In one movement, she pushed herself up. And then, standing, she held out her arms to Jonathan.

'Don't go,' she said again.

Then, as if realising what had happened, her arms dropped. She gave a little gasp, and all the colour drained from her face.

Jonathan caught her in his arms as she collapsed.

CHAPTER FIFTEEN

IT WAS only a moment before Laura's eyes opened. She looked up into Jonathan's face.

'I moved,' she said, unbelieving. 'I moved my legs, didn't I?'

Kirsty put a big cushion in behind her, for Jonathan had carried her to the couch.

Laura looked at Mark, remembering now.

'If Jonathan goes, I will go too, Mark,' she said, very steadily.

Kirsty saw the surprise on her face as Mark and Jonathan looked at each other, all hostility gone. But there was no triumph, now that their gamble had paid off, and Laura had moved her legs. There was only a united determination to do the best for the girl they both loved. And in that exchanged look Kirsty saw that a question was asked, and answered.

Jonathan nodded to Mark.

'You tell her, Mark,' he said. 'Tell her everything. She should know now.'

Mark sat down on the chair beside the couch. And then, carefully, he told Laura the whole story. How Kirsty had begun to wonder about the paralysis, with no medical reason for it, and how she had read up what she could.

'And then,' Mark said, his voice low, 'when she told me, I was so angry that I refused to consider it. It—wasn't a pleasant thought, Laura, that even unconsciously you had had to do something like this to escape from the pressures I was putting on you.'

'You weren't the only one, Mark,' Jonathan said. 'I was putting pressures on you too, Laura, and the whole thing was too much for you to handle.'

Laura looked from one to the other.

176

'Well,' she said, a little unsteadily, 'what was the next step? Oh—Dr Morton, of course.'

Mark shook his head.

'Before that,' he said, and his eyes met Kirsty's, 'I had to admit that it just could be possible. Then—yes, the next step was Dr Morton.'

He told Laura that the psychiatrist had confirmed that Laura's paralysis was a conversion reaction, and he told her of the hypnotherapy.

'And I must admit,' he said with honesty, 'that I wasn't too happy about that. Then, when Jonathan came up with this idea of us quarrelling, we checked it out with Dr Morton, and he said it was worth trying, but we weren't to be too hopeful.' His eyes met Kirsty's. 'I don't think he would have agreed to it if I hadn't been a doctor. But when you collapsed, I thought it had been a mistake to go along with it.'

A faint colour had returned to Laura's face.

'And if it hadn't worked?' she asked. 'If I had just sat there, and watched Jonathan go?'

Mark told her that if that had happened he would have stopped Jonathan at the door; he wouldn't have let him go.

'But it did work,' he said, and now Kirsty could see that the anxiety and the tension had drained from his face.

'So you're telling me that I can walk,' Laura said, very quietly. 'I'm not paralysed?'

Jonathan knelt beside the couch, and took both her hands in his.

'You are not paralysed, Laura,' he told her. 'It may take time, but you're going to get out of that chair and walk. You're going to be able to study, to do your remedial teaching, and you are going to make up your own mind about you and me. It doesn't matter what Mark wants, it doesn't matter what I want—you have all the time in the world, and you're the only one who will decide.'

Very gently, he kissed Laura's lips.

'And now,' Kirsty said, her own voice less than
steady, 'I think it's time I got a word in. Laura, you
look tired—this has all been quite a shock for you,
far too much to take in all at once. You're to say
goodnight to these two, and I'm taking you through
to bed.'

Jonathan stood up, ready to put Laura back in
her chair.

But the fair-haired girl shook her head.

'I just need to know for sure,' she said. She looked
down at her legs. It seemed to Kirsty that the whole
world was holding its breath, waiting. And then, quite
distinctly, Laura's toes wiggled. With intense concen-
tration, she lifted one leg, and then the other, off
the couch.

'One small step for Laura,' she said. 'No, it's all
right, Kirsty, I don't mean that literally; that can wait
until tomorrow. You can put me back in the chair,
Jonathan. But I'm not going to be in it for much
longer!'

She did agree, though, to be taken in the chair back
to see Dr Morton, the next day, after Mark had phoned
him. Kirsty, sitting in the waiting-room, unable to
believe how slowly the clock was moving, was startled
to hear Laura laughing as the door eventually opened
and Dr Morton pushed the wheelchair over to Kirsty.

Kirsty looked at Laura's flushed cheeks and then at
the doctor.

'What was the joke?' she said to Laura.

'I walk like a drunk man,' Laura told her. 'I took
two steps, and Dr Morton had to catch me, but it's
a start, Kirsty. Tomorrow it will be three, or
maybe four!'

On the drive home, she told Kirsty that this visit
had been completely on the level.

'I suppose you could say Dr Morton managed to get
me to let it all hang out,' she said. 'He says mine was
a fairly straightforward neurosis; because he was told
the facts, he didn't have to drag them out of me. And

he says, too, that he wasn't at all sure Jonathan's idea would work, but he felt it was worth trying, because the longer I thought I couldn't walk, the longer it would be before he could hope to make a breakthrough.'

She turned to Kirsty, and Kirsty could see the determination on her face.

'And from now on,' she said, very quietly, 'I'm going to make some progress every day. Even if it's only a little. Dr Morton says there's no reason why I shouldn't, because thanks to the physiotherapy, and the massage, and the exercises, my muscles are fine.'

The physiotherapy treatments continued, and now Meg Russell had Laura holding on to the parallel bars every day, her legs, no longer useless, moving, taking a little more weight, becoming stronger. In the swimming-pool, Laura and Kirsty did exercises twice a day, and soon Laura was doing without the small board she had been leaning on, and Kirsty could see that the gentle leg movements were becoming firmer each day. And, as Laura had said, each day she managed to walk a few steps further, first with Kirsty or Mark or Jonathan supporting her, and then on her own.

I can't believe it, Mark often found himself thinking, seeing Laura's steady progress, just a little each day, but always maintained. The bleak hopelessness of the long weeks since Laura's accident almost seemed like a bad dream.

But no dream, he would sometimes think, soberly reminding himself of all that he had learned, about himself, about his sister. And, of course, about Kirsty.

As he rang the bell at Ken and Greta Harris's house—his last house call, but he always liked to have plenty of time with them—he knew that tonight Kirsty would want to know how they were doing, facing up to Ken's multiple sclerosis.

It was Ken himself who came to the door, slowly, leaning now on two sticks. But he was positive and cheerful, Mark saw right away. Accepting of what this disease would do, but yet not giving in to it any more than he had to.

He said as much to both Ken and Greta, sitting down with them on the pleasantly shady *stoep*.

'You've got the right attitude, both of you,' he said. 'Keep going as normally as possible, but be realistic. When it hits you, accept that a few days of bed rest will help your body to handle it.'

'I saw that, after that week in hospital,' Ken agreed. 'You were right about that, Mark; it helped me and it helped Greta.' For a moment, a little awkwardly, his hand covered his wife's. 'We're not quite at the wheelchair stage, but we reckon we can face up to that when it happens, can't we, love?'

At the door, Greta asked steadily if Mark would let her have the phone number of the support society he had mentioned.

'I thought we could manage on our own, but I see now we can use all the help there is,' she admitted. She managed to smile. 'Any other tips to help us cope?'

'You're doing very well,' Mark said, meaning it. 'Just remember, Ken's physical abilities can vary from day to day. Take each day as it comes. Try not to let him be exposed to colds, infections—stress of any kind, physical or emotional. I think you'll find the support society helpful—I'll let you have their phone number.'

There was just time, he thought as he parked his car, to go up to the small hospital of the clinic, where Mrs Wingate was recovering from her bypass operation.

As he had hoped, the operation had been straightforward and successful, and already Mrs Wingate was sitting up in bed, asking when she could go home.

'I'm not the one who decides that,' he reminded her. 'You're in Dr Nathan's hands. 'And then, relenting, he said, 'But I don't think he'll keep you in much longer.'

'I feel so much better,' Mrs Wingate told him. 'I

only realise now that I was always a little tired, a little breathless. Now, even just walking around here, I feel different.'

'How is your leg?' Mark asked, for the bypass operation had used a small section of vein from Mrs Wingate's leg.

'Feels fine,' his patient assured him. 'I did tell you we have a new grandchild due in Johannesburg in two months? I've promised Margot I'll be there to help. That should be all right, shouldn't it?'

'Again, that's up to Dr Nathan—I know he will want you on his exercise programme right away—but if you go on doing as well as this I don't think he'll object.'

He stood up.

'I see they're just bringing you a cup of tea—time for me to be off anyway. I'll look back in tomorrow.'

And if the angiogram hadn't been done, and showed up the obstruction, he thought as he went along the corridor to his own rooms, I don't know if Mrs Wingate would be making plans to see her new grandchild.

As always, his waiting-room was full, and he gave a general greeting as he went through.

'First patient, Trudy,' he told his receptionist as he hurried past her desk.

A week or two later, Kirsty went through to Stellenbosch to visit little Thandi in hospital. Her tonsillectomy had had to be postponed again, because of an infection, but finally it had been done.

She was sitting up in bed in the children's ward, beaming, when Kirsty went to see her.

'This is Dr Mark's hospital, did you know that?' she said importantly. 'Dr Mark comes up every day to see me. He helped the man who took my tonsils out—I s'pose he isn't very good at it; that's why he needed Dr Mark to help him.'

'I suppose so,' Kirsty agreed gravely.

She gave the little girl the doll she had brought her,

and agreed with Thandi that the nicest of all her clothes were the frilly panties.

'Laura is going to make some more clothes for your doll when you come home,' she told the little girl. 'And Sarah says she'll knit her a warm jersey for when it's winter.'

When the bell rang for the end of visiting time, she hugged Thandi, and promised to come to the crèche to see all the children.

'Bye, Nurse Kirsty,' Thandi called, when Kirsty turned at the door and waved. And as Kirsty walked along the corridor she could hear Thandi's clear little voice telling everyone that 'that's my friend, Nurse Kirsty'.

There was just time to post her letter home, Kirsty decided. It would have to be weighed, because there had been far too much to tell to be contained in an airmail form. Laura walking, and soon to start her studying, the wine harvest, the visit they were planning down the coast, near Cape Point.

She came out of the post office and put her sunglasses on again—just in time to see Helen Shaw, posting letters in the red box.

'Oh—Kirsty, how fortunate to see you,' Helen said.

Kirsty's thoughts whirled.

Fortunate? What could Mark's ex-fiancée mean?

'I was just going back to the car,' she said warily.

'Nonsense,' Helen said firmly. 'Come and have a cup of coffee first. Or should it be tea at this time?'

There were tables under bright umbrellas just along the street, and somehow Kirsty found herself being led there. And she heard herself saying, a little faintly, that tea would be fine.

'I believe you had a little break at Malalozi,' Helen said, when the waitress had brought their tea. 'Marvellous place, isn't it?'

'Yes, it is,' Kirsty agreed.

Of course, she thought, I should have known that Helen must have been there, with Mark. Not that it mattered, but—was that why Helen had brought her here, to make the point?

But it didn't seem so, for Helen had moved away from Malalozi, very smoothly, and was talking about Laura.

'I hear she's walking again,' Helen said. 'That must be a great relief for Mark, and for that young man Mark disapproves of so much.'

Kirsty put her cup down on the table.

'Mark and Jonathan are getting to know each other now,' she said flatly.

'How very nice for everyone,' Helen replied. 'More tea? No? Well, Kirsty, before you hurry off—and I can see you're about to do that—I wanted to tell you something. I'm getting engaged. To Brent Conran. Mark and Laura know him; he's a lawyer. It will be announced in the weekend paper, but I wanted Mark to know first. And you.'

'Me?' Kirsty said, unable to hide her surprise.

'Yes, Kirsty,' Helen returned, and there was cool amusement on her beautiful face. 'Because I rather think it's very important to both you and Mark.'

Kirsty was silent, thrown by this.

'My dear,' Helen said lightly, 'I'm not blind; I realised it was a very strong possibility that Mark would turn to you after we—after I broke our engagement. I wish you joy of the sort of life that's much too demanding for me. But after all, I suppose you nurses are used to it.'

'I suppose we are,' Kirsty agreed gravely. But deep inside her there was a bubble of laughter rising, and she had to wait until she and Helen had parted, and she was safely round the corner, before she could give way to it. It wasn't really that Helen had said anything so funny, she told herself, when she was back in the car and driving back to the farm; perhaps it was as much relief as anything.

And she could see the same relief on Mark's face when she told him that night.

'He's a nice fellow, Brent,' Mark said. 'Moves in the right social circles, keeps sensible hours—yes, I think he and Helen will do very nicely together. He can be a bit correct, a bit stuffy, but maybe Helen won't mind that.'

Kirsty looked at him from under her lashes.

'And I suppose you're anything but stuffy yourself?' she asked him demurely.

'Anything but,' Mark assured her. 'And I'm not too bothered about doing the right thing, either. Which is why I want to take you to a cottage at The Boulders this weekend. Just the two of us. Any objections?'

The cottage belonged to a doctor friend, Mark told her when they were driving down the peninsula towards Cape Point on Friday evening.

'We have two whole days here, with no telephone, no obligations,' he said, drawing up beside the small stone cottage which stood sturdily just above the beach.

There was magic here too, Kirsty thought the next morning, different magic from the game reserve, but still magic—the sea, still and blue even in the early morning, the red of the rising sun, and the golden beach, with the huge boulders that gave this place its name.

They had cooked chops and sausages, the night before, on the brick *braaivleis* outside the cottage. Sarah had sent potato salad and coleslaw with them, and some of her *melktert*, and after they had eaten they had walked along the beach in the moonlight, hand in hand, not saying anything, not needing to say anything.

Then, when they'd got back to the cottage, and seen the welcoming light, Mark had stopped, and drawn her into his arms.

'There are two rooms, if you want,' he'd said, not quite steadily, looking down at her, one finger tracing the outline of her face, of her lips.

Kirsty had shaken her head.

'I want to be with you, Mark,' she'd told him, and then, with honesty, 'I thought that was why we came here.'

Mark had laughed, his dark head thrown back.

'Kirsty, my dear, darling girl, I love you.'

And then the laughter was gone, and his eyes were very dark. It was the first time he had said the words. She had known it, but it had meant so much to hear him say it.

'And I love you, Mark,' she'd said.

His arms were warm around her, and his lips demanding. Demanding a response she could give, now, with all her heart.

They'd gone inside, and Mark had closed the door.

Once, during the night, Kirsty had woken up to find the moonlight streaming into the room. Mark was asleep, and she'd leaned on one elbow and looked down at him. He looked younger, more vulnerable, somehow, when he was asleep. Unable to stop herself, she'd touched his bare brown shoulder, very gently.

He'd opened his eyes and, without a word, taken her in his arms again. And she'd known that that was exactly what she had wanted to happen.

It was only when they were on their way home that Mark said, glancing at her, 'You know, we haven't made any plans, and that was something I meant to do this weekend.'

'Was it?' Kirsty asked him. 'I thought you'd done all you planned to.'

'Not quite,' Mark replied, and he smiled. 'For instance, I don't recall that I actually asked you to marry me. Did I?'

'I don't think you did,' Kirsty told him. 'Not in so many words, anyway.'

His hand covered hers for a moment.

'I'm asking you now, Kirsty. Will you marry me?'

'Oh, yes, Mark,' Kirsty murmured unevenly. 'Oh, yes.'

'As soon as possible,' Mark told her.

'You're being bossy again,' Kirsty pointed out, but she couldn't help smiling as she said it. And then, a little uncertainly, she said, 'Mark, could we be married in Scotland? I'd like that, and my folks would like it. Actually, I don't know if my mother would ever forgive us if we got married here.'

'Of course we can,' Mark said. On one condition—that I don't have to wear a kilt!'

'You couldn't even if you wanted to,' Kirsty told him. 'You have to have the right to wear the kilt.'

'You mean I haven't told you about my grandmother Agnes Macpherson?' Mark said, surprise in his voice.

It took Kirsty a moment to realise that he was teasing her. And this, she realised, was a side of Mark that was just sort of breaking free. His life had been pretty serious, she reminded herself, left with the responsibility for the wine farm, and for his young sister, and then his years of studying, before going into private practice.

We'll laugh together, she thought.

They told Laura right away, and that night Kirsty phoned her folks to tell them.

'No,' she said firmly to Mark, 'we're not to phone until the cheap rates come on. My father would be horrified if we did. And it's a real waste of money, when all we have to do is wait a few hours.'

Fortunately, the line was clear. As clear, Kirsty thought in wonder, as if I were phoning them from Edinburgh instead of from the other side of the world. Her mother cried, and Kirsty cried, and after that Mark talked to her father, and then Kirsty's mother came back on, this time with a notebook, ready to make a list.

'In a month?' she said, horrified. 'How can I get everything ready in a month? What about your dress?'

'I'll bring it with me,' Kirsty told her, for she and Laura had already talked about that. 'One of the women on the farm will make it for me. Zita's friend Esther—remember Zita, who had the baby? And

Mum—we want the wedding to be as small as possible, just family and close friends. Oh, and Mark says will Gavin be his best man?'

Her mother, she could hear, was in tears again.

'That's so nice of Mark, and him not even knowing Gavin yet,' she managed to say. 'Kirsty, have you thought about the reception?'

'No, I haven't,' Kirsty admitted cheerfully. 'You just organise it, Mum. I'll phone again in a few days, in case there's anything we have to clear up.'

And of course there would be, she told Mark, putting the phone down.

The time was too short for Kirsty to do anything about a job, but she told Mark firmly that when they came back she would want to do some real nursing.

'I'm needing to get back into hospital work,' she said.

'Well, we're always short-staffed; I could speak to the board,' Mark promised. He hesitated, and then a little too casually said, 'This is something we haven't even talked about. I'm all for you working for a bit, Kirsty, but I—would hope we'd be thinking about children, in a year or two?'

Kirsty assured him that she would certainly want that too.

A week later she had an interview, and it was arranged that she would start in Women's Surgical when she and Mark came back from Scotland.

Laura wasn't to come to the wedding, because she would be starting her year's course in remedial teaching at Cape Town University.

'You will be careful with all the steps?' Mark said to her, and Laura assured him that she would.

No one, looking at her now, would think she had spent all these weeks in a wheelchair, Kirsty sometimes thought. Laura wasn't at the hiking stage, but she could certainly cope with ordinary walking. She was to share a flat with her friend Jan, and she would be able to use the university bus.

'And Jonathan?' Kirsty asked her, the day before she and Mark left. 'Are you getting engaged?' She had to have another look, then, at her own ring, a family ring that had belonged to Mark and Laura's grand-mother. It was a broad gold band, with sapphires and diamonds set into it. Kirsty loved it.

Laura shook her head.

'Not yet,' she said. 'Jonathan and I both feel I have to do this first. But we'll see each other, and we'll just take it as it comes.'

And she can do that now, Kirsty thought, looking at the girl who would soon be her sister-in-law. She's strong enough, at last.

The children at the crèche had made a big wedding card for her, each child adding his or her own drawing to it.

'That's my doll what you gave me,' Thandi explained. 'And she's wearing a beautiful bride's dress.'

Kirsty hugged the little girl, and then the other chil-dren, and thanked them all.

Simon insisted on sending estate wine for the wed-ding, and he and Kirsty's father had a long talk about this on the phone.

'I've promised to visit your folks when I finally have that long backpacking holiday I'm promising myself,' he told Kirsty. 'Of course, your folks will realise then what I've been trying to get you to see—that you chose the wrong man!'

Kirsty laughed and hugged him, and assured him that she had two very pretty cousins who would be delighted to meet him.

She had her final trying-on of her dress, just before it was to be put in the special hanging cover. It was all she had dreamed of, the folds of creamy silk falling softly from the high waistline, the sleeves wide and then caught in at the wrists, the neckline low enough to show off her golden shoulders, but not so low that her mother would disapprove.

'It's perfect,' she assured Esther. 'And all these pearls on the bodice—it must have taken you hours!'

Zita came in then, with baby, and Kirsty hugged the child, and promised Zita that she would bring back a little dress with tartan on it for Sarah Kirsty.

Sarah herself, large and imposing, said goodbye to Mark and Kirsty in her kitchen, refusing to come out to the car, where Simon was loading the luggage.

'You come back soon, Kirsty,' she said fiercely, and even more fiercely to Mark, 'You look after this girl, Mark.'

Somehow, it was only when they were actually in the plane, waiting for take-off, that it all became completely real for Kirsty.

I'm going home to Scotland, to be married, she thought. And—and then I'm coming back here, and this will be home.

Mark fastened his seatbelt and then turned to her.

'Your folks will come out to visit us, *meisie*,' he said, and his immediate understanding brought a tightness to her throat. 'As often as possible. Will you be homesick, Kirsty?'

'Probably a wee bit, sometimes,' Kirsty said honestly. 'But you know how we Scots have always had this pioneering spirit—I'll be all right, Mark. Because I'll be with you.'

The plane taxied out on to the runway, and began to gather speed. The wheels left the ground, and as the plane banked both Kirsty and Mark turned for the last sight of Cape Town, and Table Mountain.

Mark's hand held Kirsty's firmly.

When I come back, Kirsty thought with a deep contentment, I will be Mark's wife.

GET 4 BOOKS
AND A MYSTERY GIFT

Return this coupon and we'll send you 4 Love on Call novels and a mystery gift absolutely FREE! We'll even pay the postage and packing for you.

We're making you this offer to introduce you to the benefits of Reader Service: FREE home delivery of brand-new Love on Call novels, at least a month before they are available in the shops, FREE gifts and a monthly Newsletter packed with information.

Accepting these FREE books and gift places you under no obligation to buy, you may cancel at any time, even after receiving just your free shipment. Simply complete the coupon below and send it to:

HARLEQUIN MILLS & BOON, FREEPOST, PO BOX 70, CROYDON, CR9 9EL.

No stamp needed

Yes, please send me 4 free Love on Call novels and a mystery gift. I understand that unless you hear from me, I will receive 4 superb new titles every month for just £1.99* each postage and packing free. I am under no obligation to purchase any books and I may cancel or suspend my subscription at any time, but the free books and gifts will be mine to keep in any case. (I am over 18 years of age)

1EP5D

Ms/Mrs/Miss/Mr _____

Address _____

_____

_____ Postcode _____

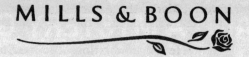

MILLS & BOON

LOVE ON CALL

The books for enjoyment this month are:

TAKEN FOR GRANTED	Caroline Anderson
HELL ON WHEELS	Josie Metcalfe
LAURA'S NURSE	Elisabeth Scott
VET IN DEMAND	Carol Wood

Treats in store!

Watch next month for the following absorbing stories:

IMPOSSIBLE SECRET	Margaret Barker
A PRACTICE MADE PERFECT	Jean Evans
WEDDING SONG	Rebecca Lang
THE DECIDING FACTOR	Laura MacDonald